PRAISE FOR THE MADISON NIGHT MYSTERY SERIES

"A terrific mystery is always in fashion—and this one is sleek, chic and constantly surprising. Vallere's smart styling and wry humor combine for a fresh and original page-turner—it'll have you eagerly awaiting her next appealing adventure. I'm a fan!"

— Hank Phillippi Ryan,
Agatha, Anthony, Macavity and Mary Higgins Clark Award-Winning Author of *The Other Woman*

"All of us who fell in love with Madison Night in *Pillow Stalk* will be rooting for her when the past comes back to haunt her in *That Touch of Ink*. The suspense is intense, the plot is hot and the style is to die for. A thoroughly entertaining entry in this enjoyable series."

— Catriona McPherson,
Agatha Award-Winning Author of the Dandy Gilver Mystery Series

"A fast-paced mystery with fab fashions, an appealing heroine, and a clever twist, *That Touch of Ink* is especially for fans of all things mid-century modern."

— *ReadertoReader.com*

"Vallere has crafted an extremely unique mystery series with an intelligent heroine whose appeal will never go out of style."

– *Kings River Life Magazine*

"Diane Vallere…has a wonderful touch, bringing in the design elements and influences of the '50s and '60s era many of us hold dear while keeping a strong focus on what it means in modern times to be a woman in business for herself, starting over."

— *Fresh Fiction*

"A humorous yet adventurous read of mystery, very much worth considering."

— Paul Vogel,
Midwest Book Review

"Make room for Vallere's tremendously fun homage. Imbuing her story with plenty of mid-century modern decorating and fashion tips…Her disarmingly honest lead and two hunky sidekicks will appeal to all fashionistas and antiques types and have romance crossover appeal."

— *Library Journal*

"The writing was crisp with a solid plot that kept me engaged with Madison, Tex and the other supporting cast." — *Dru's Book Musing*

"The strength of this series that Madison has changed, adapted, and grown over the course of the six books." — *3 no 7 Looks at Books*

TEACHER'S THREAT

A Madison Night Mystery

TEACHER'S THREAT

A Madison Night Mystery

Diane Vallere

POLYESTER PRESS BOOKS

TEACHER'S THREAT

Madison Night Mad for Mod Mystery #8

A Polyester Press Mystery

Polyester Press

www.polyesterpress.com

This is a work of fiction. Characters, places, and events are the product of the author's imagination or are used fictitiously. Any resemblance to real people, companies, institutions, organizations, or incidents is entirely coincidental. No affiliation with Doris Day or Paramount Studios is claimed or implied.

Cover design by Diane Vallere. Rocky (dog) Artwork © Henery Press, used with permission

eBook ISBN: 9781954579132

Paperback ISBN: 9781954579149

Hardcover ISBN: 9781954579279

❃ Created with Vellum

To anyone who has pursued a degree after the age of fifty.

"I'm sorry, Madison. You're just not good on paper."

It was, possibly, my least favorite sentence, and I'd heard versions of it from every bank in town. The loan officer for the Dallas First National Bank who had introduced himself as Pete Cross was the most recent. He smoothed his tie. It was burgundy, black, and cream and had a cello and musical notes as part of the otherwise abstracted pattern. He wore it with a burgundy shirt and black suit. The effect was equal parts mafia groupie and musician.

"What about the apartment building on Gaston Avenue?" I asked.

"The apartment building doesn't generate enough income to support the size of the loan you want. If you sold the building, you might have the deposit you needed. Have you considered that?"

"That's not an option."

"Is there anything else you could use as collateral? Can you sell off some inventory?"

I averted my eyes, though without a computer screen in

front of me, my options for distraction were limited. I fixated on the corner of a window on the wall behind Pete's desk. The blinds had bent, and a shaft of blinding sunlight peeked through like a special effect in a movie about hidden portals to alternate realities. I stared at the corner of sunlight for so long that when I looked back at Pete, his face was replaced with a black square, fuzzy at the edges. I blinked a few times, but it didn't help.

"I lost my inventory in a lawsuit. I've been paying rent on an empty showroom, but until I can fill it, I'm just throwing money away. Clients aren't interested in a decorator with an empty studio. I need to look like I'm back in business before I can officially get back into business."

Pete closed my shiny red folder and shook his head. "You've been lucky so far, but this," he said, tapping the closed cover, "isn't enough."

"What about letters of recommendation?" I asked.

"Letters of recommendation won't make the difference. If you have a relationship with the author, the letter's worth as much as the paper it's printed on. I'm sorry, Madison," Pete finished, "My hands are tied. If you had a business degree or a partner, things might be different. You've been lucky so far, but the bank doesn't think you're a good risk."

This, it seemed, was the popular opinion amongst the banks of the greater Dallas area: a self-taught interior designer who parlayed a love of Doris Day movies into a mid-century modern decorating business was a poor gamble. Pete was right on that count too: I didn't look good on paper.

I thanked Pete, collected my folder (now a little worse for wear), and left. At each bank, the story had been the same: in order to loan you money, you have to show us you can pay us back. I understood their reasoning, and as far as requirements to give out money, their expectations were sound. I just didn't like their lack of confidence in my abilities to do so.

I walked to my car, a vintage blue Alfa Romeo, and sat behind the wheel while considering my options. It was two thirty in the afternoon and I had nowhere to be. I'd spent my day shuttling from bank to bank hoping to charm them with my self-made success, but the plan had backfired. What had Pete just said? If I had a formal business education, things might be different.

Across the street from the Dallas First National Bank was the entrance to a private institute of higher learning. In a town that celebrated the unofficial "everything is bigger in Texas" motto, this college defied expectation by being small. Van Doren College was chiseled into concrete on four-foot-tall walls by an entrance that led to their campus. Before I knew what I was doing, I drove through the gates and parked in a visitor space outside the admissions hall. If I wanted to change minds, I was going to have to start somewhere.

Business school, here I come.

A WEEK PASSED in a flurry of applications, emails, and flat-out begging to talk my way into joining the semester in session. The dean suggested I audit the undergrad courses to get up to speed with the language of business, so I crash-coursed two weeks' worth of online courses in four days. The antidote to the resulting brain fog was a weekend binge of *The Doris Day Show.*

For my first day of school, I'd chosen a skirt suit from the wardrobe of Tootie Morgan, an elementary school teacher in the mid-sixties. She favored waist-length jackets, narrow pencil skirts, and patterned blouses. Her estate came with five bookcases filled with yearbooks; Tootie had collected one for every class she taught. When the ruling came down on my legal matter and I was forced to turn my inventory over to a competitive designer, the greatest collection of student signatures changed hands. I'd always thought they'd make a great showpiece to an educator's den, but the last I heard, they were being used to collage a bathroom at a nightclub downtown.

Van Doren College was a privately funded institution established in 1956. They had initially been an all-women's college and offered degrees in liberal arts, science, education, and business. The school maintained a competitive class size and a reputable curriculum. Instead of wooing prospective students with flashy football teams, they consistently turned out graduates who shaped the way Dallas business was done.

Aside from the dean's recommendation, I opted for in-person learning over the online experience. I've always been a hands-on person, and I doubted education would be different. I still needed a signature from the professor of Radical Business Strategy. I arrived at the college early and sought his office.

I approached a cluster of young blondes who stood on the grass out front. Halfway there, their awareness of me became obvious. They nudged one another in the way teenagers who thought they were being covert sometimes did, and the chatter of girlish conversation ceased.

"Excuse me," I said. "I'm sorry to interrupt, but do any of you know where I can find Professor Gallagher?"

The smallest of the young women, a blonde in head-to-toe black Lycra and neon pink sneakers, spoke first. "We live in the dorms," she said, which had nothing to do with my question.

"He's in his office," supplied a second blonde, this one both taller and thinner than the first. She wore a cranberry and gold sweatshirt with VDC embroidered on the front, though the garment had been cropped and the bottom halves of all the letters were missing. She pointed at the building behind me, and her sweatshirt rode up, revealing the bottom of a black sports bra. "In Canfield. He keeps office hours before and after his courses. His first class is at eight."

"Stalker much?" asked a third blonde with a snicker. The petite blonde and the other blondes laughed, and the tall blonde who had given me the comprehensive breakdown of the professor's schedule turned pink.

Living in Texas meant being fluent in blonde. That was not an indictment of blondes' intellect or an endorsement of the dumb blonde stereotype, simply an observation of the sheer number of blondes in the city. Far be it from me to criticize their choice; thanks first to genes and lately to infrequent visits to a local Dallas salon, I was one of them.

"Thank you," I said to the one who'd given me the information. I put my keys into my vintage white backpack and left them out front.

The Canfield Building wanted to make sure you never forgot where you were. Inside, a banner proclaimed, "Canfield School of Business. Where the field of business has a can-do attitude." To my immediate left was a glass display case with photos of graduates, and to my right was a school pride kiosk that displayed sweatshirts with logos not unlike the cropped one I'd seen on the tall blonde out front.

Directly in front of me was an open office where a white man in a red bowtie and blue and white checkered shirt stood next to a copy machine.

"Excuse me," I said to him. "Can you point me in the direction of Professor Gallagher's office?" I asked.

He pointed down the hall. "Third door on the left," he said. "If the door is closed, don't go in."

I glanced at the clock. "I know. He's having office hours."

"Office hours. Right." He pulled a stack of fresh copies off the machine and jammed them into a nylon messenger bag as if he were afraid I'd see what was on them. It occurred to me that if you were making a hundred copies of anything, you likely expected to distribute them for publicity, which made his clandestine action counterproductive.

I thanked the man and followed his directions. My sneakers were silent against the linoleum tile, which made it easy to overhear raised voices. The closer I got, the clearer it was that the voices came from Professor Gallagher's office. The door was closed. I hesitated. A door slammed, and then there was silence. I waited awkwardly, and then knocked.

A moment later, a male voice said, "Come in."

I opened the door. Behind the desk sat a man in his forties. He had brown hair, a gray beard, and an off-season tan. He wore a white polo under a dark gray jacket.

"Professor Gallagher?" I asked. "I'm Madison Night. I'm an MBA candidate. I need your signature to enroll in your Radical Business Strategy course." My voice trailed off while I waited for a sign that the man was who I thought he was. Aside from "Come in," he'd been awkwardly silent. Awkward for me, that is. He seemed perfectly at home despite having been interrupted.

"Close the door behind you. Sit down." I entered and pulled my paperwork out of my backpack. He held his hand up. "I'm not going to sign it," he said.

"Why not?"

"Because you're late. My class started weeks ago, and you'll never get caught up."

"With all due respect, Professor, I have business experience, and I'm a quick study. I've spent the past week auditing foundational business courses, and so far I've learned nothing new."

He tipped his chair back and moved his elbows to the armrests on his chair. His fingers remained threaded and rested on his midsection. "What business experience do you have?"

"I'm a decorator."

He leaned forward, picked up his pen, and resumed whatever task he'd been working on. It was as if I weren't there. He glanced up at me and pointed at the door. "You can go now. Radical Business Strategy isn't for you."

His dismissal wasn't my first, but it was my most recent. Piled on top of the recent bank rejections, and I'd had just about enough of men in authority telling me what was right for me. I stood and moved my backpack to the chair and then put my palms on the edge of the professor's desk and leaned toward him.

"For the past decade, I've owned a decorating firm. I specialize in mid-century modern design, which I learned from studying Doris Day movies. I have acquired inventory at a fraction of its price by reading the obituaries, identifying women of a certain age, and contacting their next of kin. You would be surprised how many people my age lack nostalgia when money is involved."

He set down his pen and leaned back again. "Who taught you to do that?"

"Aside from the experience I picked up working for a decorator in Pennsylvania over a decade ago, I taught myself everything I know. I've made contacts with funeral homes, powder coaters, and trash men. My business has posted double- and triple-digit increases since I opened. I've had an offer from one of the most successful architects in Dallas that I turned down because I liked working for myself."

"What happened?"

"What do you mean?"

"You sound like you have a good thing going, but you're here at a college, well past an age when most people attend." He held up his hand. "No offense, but you're not exactly a schoolgirl."

This was what I thought of as a Doris Day moment. How often did people think they knew who, or what, she was? How many times did people write her off as fluff and then learn she was smart, talented, funny, and sexy? How much time would she have wasted if she got angry every time they did?

I forced a smile and softened my voice. "Professor Gallagher. I believe I can learn something new from your course, and I believe my experience might inspire your students. Starting my company wasn't easy, but I persisted, and I'm prepared to do that again." I pulled the paperwork out of my backpack, unfolded the documents, and set them in front of him. I picked up his pen and turned it around and extended it. "If you want me to go away, all you have to do is sign. Let me decide if Radical Business Strategy is right for me."

For longer than felt comfortable, we remained in that position: me extending his pen, him sitting back with his hands folded across his midsection. Out of my peripheral vision, I saw the rise and fall of my chest with each breath. My palms dampened with sweat and my pulse thudded in my neck. The hint of a cramp announced itself behind my right shoulder blade.

"That was a pop quiz. You passed." He took the pen. He signed the paperwork. He set the pen down and handed me the pages. "Be in class tomorrow morning at eight," he said. "Room 102. I can't say you'll survive, but it will be fun watching you try."

2

I LEFT THE OFFICE ON UNSTABLE LEGS. I'D EXPECTED A professorial type: tweed suit, studious attitude. An interest in finding a student who had an almost passionate desire to learn. I'd expected him to hear my request, ask a few polite questions, ignore my age, and sign my paperwork.

But Professor Gallagher was like an attack dog protecting his curriculum. He dismissed me before asking about my motivation. Perhaps that was lesson number one: don't wait to be asked what you want. Class didn't start until tomorrow, but I'd consider it a freebie.

THE NEXT MORNING, I dressed in a green Banlon top with white flowers appliqued to the hem and a coordinating white skirt with green flowers. I attached a white metal daisy pin close to my collar and slipped on a pair of green and pink flowered canvas Keds. Too much. I swapped the sneakers out for white and tied a Vera scarf around the handle of my backpack.

I drove to the campus, parked in Lot B, and made it to room 102 of the Canfield Building in seven minutes. The door was open, and students milled around inside, chatting amongst themselves in clusters around the room. I stood by the chalkboard. RISK was scrolled in large letters across the surface.

"You should have told me you're the new teaching assistant," said a man next to me. "I could have warned you."

I turned to face the young man I'd seen behind the admissions desk yesterday. Today his bowtie was navy with pink and white stripes. "Warned me about what?" I asked.

"Gallagher's no picnic. You'll see." The man scanned the room and then returned his attention to me. "If you do what he asks and knock ten"—he stepped back and assessed me from head to toe—"maybe twenty years off your age, you'll be fine. The last TA was fired after meeting with students behind his back. They said they were afraid to approach him. Gallagher said if students are scared of him, they'd never make it in business." He walked away.

The tall blonde who had directed me to Gallagher's office made her way toward me. "Hi," she said. "I'm Faye. I heard you tell Eric you were the new TA."

"I'm Madison," I said. "But I think there's been some mistake. I'm not—"

She grabbed my hand and pumped it. "You have no idea how happy I am to meet you."

Before I could correct her misassumption, we were interrupted by a door slamming shut. Everyone in the class got quiet, and Professor Gallagher walked to the front of the room. When he reached the desk, he sat on the corner and made a show of looking at each individual face. I hadn't chosen a seat yet, and from my standing vantage point, I could easily see which students were comfortable and which ones wanted to hide.

Gallagher's sight eventually rested on me. I smiled and held my backpack with both hands. "Please, Ms. Night, don't stand on my account. Take a seat. Any seat. I suppose you can't take any seat because you let the others take theirs first." He shook his head at my lack of initiative. "It seems you've got a choice between the one directly in front of me, which somehow is always vacant, and the one closest to the door, which incidentally is also always vacant. Which will it be?"

There was no mistaking the taunt in his voice. Getting him to sign my papers wasn't an accomplishment. It was bait. I had no idea what went into Radical Business Strategy, but public humiliation appeared to be part of it.

I passed the vacant seat by the door and walked to the front of the room. I stopped and smiled at the professor and then lowered myself into the seat directly in front of him. I pulled a notebook and pen out of my backpack and slid the pack under my chair.

He nodded his head at me. "Let's start with a case study," he said to the class. "A moderately successful decorator loses her business after being sued for fraud. She loses her inventory, her client list, and her line of credit with the bank. In a week, she's paying rent on an empty storefront. Banks turn down her loan applications, but she's too proud to solicit money from a personal source. Where does she go from here?"

My face flushed with heat. That case study wasn't just awkwardly familiar—it was my life. In the twenty-four hours since asking Gallagher to sign off on my request to join his class, He must have read every piece of information he could find on me. I came here to learn, not be mocked. If I hadn't chosen the desk directly in front of the professor, I would have left.

"Eric, go," Gallagher said.

Eric, I discovered, was the student in the bowtie. "The decorator should apply for work with a larger firm. She has skills, but the backing of a reputable company will help offset the bad publicity."

"Who thinks that's the way to go?" the professor asked. A few hands went up. "Faye, you had your hand up. What do you think she should do?"

"She needs to get out of her lease so she's not throwing away money. Find a cheaper location. Solicit business from clients. Maybe do a big public job in exchange for free publicity."

"Who likes that idea?" he asked. Fewer hands went up this time. "Anybody else?"

A series of suggestions were called out: "Get over herself and ask friends for money," "get a co-signer," "find a new business," and "take on a partner." While I didn't love the suggestions, I appreciated that not one of them said the decorator in question should give up.

"Madison, you've been quiet," the professor said to me. "What do you think the decorator should do?"

He already knew I didn't know the answer. If I did, I wouldn't be in his class. But something about Professor Gallagher got my goat. Admitting I didn't have the answer felt like giving in, and giving in felt like giving up. Mad for Mod defined me. It didn't matter how many decorating firms existed in Dallas or how niche the mid-century modern market was. I was the best at it, and giving it up wasn't an option.

"She should expand," I said coolly. The professor raised his eyebrows. "She did remarkably well for several years, and that was on instinct. First she needs to shore up her business plan so the banks know she's a good risk. That might require some outside education. She needs to go big with a loan so she can invest in inventory, advertising, and client outreach all at once. Keep the current office but look for additional property. A satellite office. Double down on what she does best and be ruthless with jobs that don't fit her specialty."

"Are you nuts?" Eric called out. "Who's going to hire a decorator that steals ideas?"

I turned toward him. "There were extenuating circumstances," I said. "People will understand." I hadn't expected to respond out loud, and as I heard what I said replayed in my head, I added, "Probably."

Professor Gallagher continued. "Good points. Anybody who followed the news knows she was found guilty, which will make potential clients think twice about engaging her services. Is Madison's point germane? Does it matter why she did it?"

"Yes," I said. "It's an explanation. People like human interest stories, and hers is unique."

"How would you know?" Eric asked.

I turned to face Gallagher. "Tell him," he instructed.

I turned back to Eric and the other students. "I know because I'm the decorator."

A ripple ran through the other students. It sounded like locusts. My cheeks flushed again. Eric glowered at me. I turned my back on the rest of my class and stared straight ahead, focusing on a piece of chalk that rested in the tray below the chalk board.

Gallagher saw an opening for theatrics. "Ladies and Gentlemen, meet Madison Night," he said, gesturing to me. "She's the owner of Mad for Mod, a boutique decorating firm on Greenville Avenue, and she's your newest classmate. Yesterday, Madison told me she posted double- and triple-digit increases since opening, won a county-wide decorating competition that expanded her client base overnight, and has turned down offers to buy her business. She did not tell me she operated with zero debt on her balance sheet." He shifted his attention from the rest of the class to me. "Why didn't you tell me that?"

"It didn't seem relevant," I said.

"It's very relevant," he said.

The professor turned his back on the class and went to the chalkboard. He underlined RISK. "If you want to succeed, you have to get comfortable with risk. You have to learn to think you know nothing. Less than nothing. You have to do the opposite of every instinct you have." He looked at me. "Madison's answer was filled with risk. She lost her business, but think about the words she used: expand. Go big. Double down. Invest." He ticked them off on his fingers. "Those are power words. They're the concepts we need to use every day." He looked at the class. "If I didn't believe her answer was fueled by anger at me, I'd say she did a very good job."

The class rippled again. Laughing locusts.

The next hour was filled with heated discussions about my situation. Had I left, I would have missed out on one of the most productive brainstorming sessions of my life. I might not have liked how Professor Gallagher initiated the subject, but I couldn't deny the results.

When class ended, a rush of students approached the professor. "Faye, stay after class," he said. "Everybody else, office hours are at four-six."

I led the group out of the classroom. A few people welcomed me to the shark tank. No one asked me to join them for lunch in the quad, but it still felt like a victory.

THREE CLASSES INTO MY SCHEDULE, it was obvious Radical Business Strategy would be the highlight of my semester. Accounting and Operations Process were easy; I'd been doing my accounting from the beginning, and as a sole proprietor, I wrote the operations manual. My one part-time employee was a business school student herself, but her contribution to the Mad for Mod Operations had been a cloud-based system to track my inventory, which had simply streamlined the process of producing an itemized list after the lawsuit went south. She also introduced me to hug therapy, which (so far) I hadn't seen mentioned on the Van Doren curriculum.

At six forty-five, after a full day of classes, I returned to the admissions desk. Eric was behind the desk like he'd been that morning. He scowled when he saw me. "You're wasting your time," he said. "Gallagher won't change the way he treats you in class. He's like that with everybody."

"That's good. I don't want him to change his style of teaching on my account."

"You don't care that he made a fool of you in class?"

Was that how it looked? I reflected on the moment. Yes, I'd felt embarrassed at first. I'd wanted to crawl into my vintage white backpack and hide. The mistake I'd made had cost me more than I thought I could lose, and the professor had pulled at that thread like he was deconstructing a vintage needlepoint.

"Sure, it was humiliating at first, but that was because I tried to keep my failure a secret and he confronted it straight-away. Once it was out in the open and the class brainstormed solutions, I got over my embarrassment and started thinking about where to go next."

"It's like I said in class," Eric said. "If you want to rebound, you should take a job at a big company. That's the real way forward." He slammed a book and put it on a shelf. "Or keep plugging away in the land of small potatoes. That's where small minds are most comfortable."

What a jerk.

I shook my head and walked down the hall to Professor Gallagher's office. Voices poured from inside. Angry voices.

I waited in the hallway for him to finish with whoever was with him. As I got closer, the voices subsided. I hesitated, waiting for the door to open and a student to exit.

Instead, I heard a gunshot.

3

A MOMENT AFTER THE SHOT, A DOOR SLAMMED. I TURNED THE doorknob and the door swung inward. I braced myself for what I might find: body, blood, weapon. I found option D: none of the above.

"Hello," said a man behind the desk. He reached forward and clicked Pause on the remote. From the frozen image, I recognized Samuel Jackson and John Travolta from *Pulp Fiction*. This wasn't the scene in which they discussed the Royale with Cheese.

The man held a pipe in one hand and a dingy, rag in the other. When I entered, he set both down. He held one hand up with his index finger extended and wiggled it in my direction. "Let me guess. You're not one of the parents. . . maybe a new professor? No. Drama coach." His eyes moved from my face to my outfit. "Wardrobe? Yes. They did say they were bringing in an outside party, though I hardly expected you to come see me before rehearsal." He stood. "Ansel Benedict," he said. "Or should I say Henry Higgins? I've just been cast as the lead in the North Dallas production of *My Fair Lady.*"

He bowed, less at-your-service and more encore-encore.

"Did I hear a gun?" I asked.

Ansel reached into a desk drawer and pulled out a pistol with black electrical tape wound around the handle. I stepped back and held my hands up. He laughed.

"Starter's pistol," he said. He opened the pistol and emptied out the blanks. He closed it and set in his open palm and served it to me as if it were a tray of appetizers. As he moved it around, I could tell the handle under the tape was bright orange. I looked back at Ansel.

"I took a bit of a liberty today. *Pulp Fiction* always gets my blood going. You understand, I'm sure."

I didn't. "I'm looking for Professor Gallagher," I said. "Isn't this his office?"

"Yes and no. This is his office, but you won't find him here. My office is in the Dramatic Arts building. A pipe burst, and until the work is complete, Gallagher and I are temporary roommates. I'm sure you can understand how difficult it is to concentrate with business majors running around all the time." He waved his hand as if shooing away a fly. He paused to consider something, and his thick eyebrows pulled together like a bold black underline below his forehead. "Has the college given you an office? I don't suppose they would, you being temporary. I'd say you can borrow mine from time to time, but as I've said, it's unavailable."

"I think you misunderstand who I am." I held out a hand. "Madison Night."

I didn't think it was possible for Ansel's eyebrows to get any closer, but at the mention of my name, they appeared to overlap. He seemed put off by both my name and my outstretched hand. To his credit, he did stand and take my fingertips in his, though it could hardly count as a handshake.

He dropped my hand and fished a handkerchief out of his pants pocket to wipe off my cooties (I surmised).

He lowered himself back into Professor Gallagher's chair. "I don't suppose you are the costumer for *My Fair Lady*, are you?"

"No. I'm an MBA candidate."

"Well, then our business here is done."

"Mine isn't. I have outstanding questions about this morning's lecture."

"And this is my problem how?"

"It's not your problem, it's mine. It's why I'm here for Professor Gallagher's office hours."

"Yes, Professor Gallagher loves to help the students." If Ansel Benedict were trying to hide his dislike of the business professor, he was failing miserably. "He especially likes to help after class. He likely could, and would, and will." He sighed in great dramatic form. "Just not here and not now." He picked up the handset and pressed four numbers in rapid succession. "It's Ansel. Eliza Doolittle is here to see you. Where shall I send her?" He paused for an answer. "I'll relay the message." He hung up. "William just left for the day. If you scurry away like a good little flower girl, you might catch him in the parking structure."

It took a moment to realize in Ansel's world, everyone was a character. I thanked the aspiring actor and left him to his pipe cleaning or his pistol firing or whatever scene he was about to work on next. As I retraced my steps to the front office, I glanced behind the desk. Eric was gone, and the door behind the office was ajar.

"Hello?" I called. "Is anyone here?" There was no answer. For as active as the quad was in the afternoon, after six

Canfield had all the hallmarks of a building evacuated for demolition.

I left the building. The blondes were where they'd been yesterday morning. I smiled in their direction, and two smiled back. I walked to the lot where I'd parked my car. It was parked next to a small, gray Fiat, and Professor Gallagher stood between them.

"Professor," I called out as I approached. "I was just looking for you."

"Not now," he snapped. He put his hands on the roof of the car and leaned down, staring into the back. He yanked on the driver's side door, but it was locked. He cursed. He straightened up and walked around the back of the Fiat to the passenger side. Whatever he saw there made him curse again.

"Is something wrong?" I asked.

"My car was broken into." He pulled out his phone and called the campus police. After giving his name and number, he described the situation. "This is Professor Gallagher. I'm parked in Lot B. Yep. Same method. Sure. I'll wait." He hung up. "Third time this month."

As I got closer, I could see inside the Fiat. The backseat was filled with notebooks, and loose papers were scattered about. "Did you lock it?" I asked.

"Of course, I locked it." He gestured for me to join him outside the passenger-side door. I circled the back of the car and noticed a four-inch gap between the top of the door and the frame of the car. It was just about wide enough to feed a narrow hand through.

"How did that happen?"

"It was done with an entry airbag. Locksmiths carry them. It looks like a heavy duty balloon. You feed it, deflated, into the gap between the door and the car and pump it up. The pressure from the airbag forces the door to bend away from the car far enough so someone can reach in and unlock the door by hand."

"But it doesn't go back to normal after the airbag is deflated," I guessed.

"Right. The damage is minimal if the airbag is used correctly, because as soon as the door is away from the frame, the car can be unlocked. This," he pointed to his car, "was not used correctly. Now the door won't close properly."

My natural curiosity kicked in. I peered closer at the car. "Does insurance cover something like this?"

"I have a five-hundred-dollar deductible, and the part costs twelve hundred. The mechanic bent it back with his hands in under five minutes."

"Then it's an easy fix."

"Not quite. Every time he bends it, the hinges weaken. Pretty soon they'll break."

A campus police officer arrived via golf cart. He was late twenties, dressed in a uniform of gray short-sleeved shirt, black pants, and baseball hat. The shirt had a patch on the sleeve that said Campus Security above Van Doren College. The same two lines of text were embossed on his shirt directly above the left breast pocket. His ID was clipped to the right. I didn't know much about the qualifications required to become a campus police officer, but he didn't appear to be armed.

The officer parked the golf cart several feet away from us and climbed out. He nodded at me and then approached the professor. The men discussed the situation: same MO as before, nothing seemed to be missing, an inconvenience at best. There was no reason to stay, but after months of having little of interest in my life, I felt a thrill at being this close to something eventful. I hovered and eavesdropped.

"Is anything missing?" the CP asked.

"Hard to say," the professor answered. "I had the course files for night school back there along with last semester's final projects and some case studies."

"Looks to me like vandalism. Somebody wanted to mess with a professor, and your car was the target." The CP looked at me. "Did your car get broken into too?"

"No," I said.

"Do you still think this was random?" the professor asked the CP. "Three separate times?"

"We've seen things like this before." The campus policeman didn't seem overly concerned by the vandalism. "Could be someone wasn't happy with his grade. Or could be a prank. Either way, you might want to start locking your files in your trunk."

Professor Gallagher seemed unsatisfied by the theory. The campus policeman climbed back into his golf cart and drove off. It didn't feel like the right time to engage the professor in a discussion of business, but it didn't feel like the right time to hop in my car and drive off either.

"Can I give you a ride someplace?"

He was half inside the car, corralling errant papers together. He shoved a pile into a cardboard box, lifted it out, and set it on the macadam. "Help me move the files," he said. He pulled his remote out and unlocked the trunk. I joined him, and we made swift work of the task. When we were done, he slammed the trunk closed. He rested one hand on the roof of the car and appeared to be out of breath.

A moment later, he got into the car. The engine started easily. He put the car in reverse and backed slowly out of his space. The passenger-side door swung open and knocked into my Alfa Romeo.

I tapped the roof of his Fiat and bent down. The door swung open. Gallagher reached across the car and pulled it shut from the inside. It failed to latch. I tried to slam it from the outside, and it just bounced against the frame. "You'll have to secure it from the inside."

"With what?"

I pulled the daisy-printed scarf from the handle of my backpack. "Use this," I said. At his initial protest, I added, "I have more vintage scarves than you could possibly imagine."

He took the scarf. I couldn't help noticing that for all the assistance I provided, he hadn't once said thank you. What at first had appeared to be his direct teaching style seemed less welcome now that we were out of the classroom.

I stepped away from our cars and checked the time on my phone. I might miss rush-hour traffic, but I was still going to be late. I turned my back on the professor and called my dinner companion.

"Allen," Tex answered.

"It's Madison," I said.

Tex Allen was the captain of the Lakewood Police Department. We'd met under unusual circumstances, danced around an unexpected attraction for a few years, and eventually started up an unpublicized romance.

Growing anti-cop sentiment was his reason for keeping things quiet. Negative publicity from the lawsuit was mine. There was also the reality of starting a relationship in your fifties to contend with; two people, set in their ways, made for a questionable union.

After a particularly murky homicide investigation four months ago, Tex indicated he was ready to go public with the kind of grand gesture you found in romantic comedies. The ball was in my court. I was 100 percent interested and 85 percent emotionally available, though I kept that last part to myself. Once I figured out my business, I figured the final 15 percent would get on board.

"I'm going to be late," I said.

"Is it an emergency?"

"No, just an inconvenience. I stayed behind to talk to a professor." It didn't seem prudent to gossip about the vandalism while the professor was mere feet away, so I added, "I'll tell you about it later."

"Can't wait. It has to be more interesting than sensitivity training."

I chuckled. At fifty years old, Tex and I were both being schooled.

I hung up the phone and turned back to check on the professor. His Fiat was directly behind my car, and the engine was running. I bent down to see if the scarf trick had worked, but what I saw instead was the professor slumped against the dash.

4

I RAN TO THE DRIVER'S SIDE AND YANKED ON THE DOOR HANDLE. The door was locked. I knocked repeatedly, but Professor Gallagher didn't respond. I ran around to the passenger-side door. My scarf trick had worked too well; the door didn't budge.

I turned around in a full circle looking for help. "Is anyone here?" I called. My voice echoed off the cavernous parking structure. "Anyone?"

I tried the doors again and pounded my fists on the window. The professor slumped further, his head slipping to the side of the steering wheel. I had the number for campus police in my orientation package, but I'd left it sitting on my dining room table.

Not knowing the extent of the professor's unconsciousness, I took immediate actions and called 911. After providing my name and contact information, I described the situation to the dispatch officer. "I'm in parking structure B next to the Canfield Building. One of the professors is locked inside his car, and he's unconscious. He was fine a few minutes ago. I don't know what happened."

"I'll dispatch officers. Stay on the line. Can you see inside the vehicle?"

"Yes."

"Is there any evidence of drugs or a weapon?"

I bent down and peered into the passenger window. The center console was empty, and the glove box was closed.

"No," I said. "Nothing. He's slumped against the steering wheel. He backed the car out of his space and must have passed out. The car is still running but—"

She cut me off. "Have you checked the tailpipe?"

I moved to the back of the car. It was curious; the car was running, but no exhaust came out of the tailpipe. I bent at the waist and checked the pipe. Something had been jammed inside.

"The tailpipe is blocked," I said. I reached in. The metal was hot, and I recoiled.

"The EMTs are on their way."

In the distance, the sound of sirens approached. I understood the importance of leaving the car as it was. A rag in the professor's tailpipe suggested violence, not vandalism. It would be evidence.

I nervously paced behind the cars, too anxious to sit inside mine. A police car sped into the parking structure. An emergency vehicle followed. The sirens were deafening. I flagged the vehicles toward me. The ambulance parked nearest to where we stood, and two men jumped out.

I watched as they tried to open the doors the same way I had. An officer in uniform got out of his car. He took a tire iron from his trunk and approached the professor's car. He fed the end into the gap between the car and the door and leveraged it with his weight. The door bent away from the frame in the manner Professor Gallagher had described the balloon being used on the passenger-side door. The officer held the bar while an EMT reached in and unlocked the door from the inside. He then reached across the professor's body to unclip the seatbelt.

I stood several feet away. Professor Gallagher fell to the side. The EMT pulled him out. A second EMT had set up a gurney on the ground, and the two of them laid him onto it.

The uniformed officer joined me. His name, Young, was clipped to the breast pocket of his uniform, and it fit his boyish features. "Ma'am? Are you"—he checked his phone —"Madison Night?"

"Yes. I made the call."

He introduced himself. "Please step over here so I can get your statement."

I wanted to call Tex and ask what to do, but this wasn't his precinct, and I'd been through enough emergency calls to know the basic drill. I followed the officer.

"Please state your name and then tell me what happened." He held out his phone.

"Madison Night. I'm a student at the college." A flicker of surprise crossed the officer's face, but he didn't interrupt me. "My car was—is parked next to the professor's. I wanted to talk to him about our class earlier today, but he was distracted."

"The professor was conscious when you got here?"

"Yes. His car had been broken into. He said it was the third time this month. He called campus police and reported the incident. I helped him move his files to the trunk, and then he backed away to leave."

"When did he pass out?"

"I don't know, but it had to have happened in minutes. I gave him my scarf to secure the vandalized door and turned away from him to make a phone call. When I finished my conversation, I turned back and saw the car behind mine. The car was running, but the professor's body language indicated something was wrong."

"What did you do?"

"With all due respect, can't I give my statement later? The professor probably requires immediate medical attention."

One of the EMTs approached us. "Notify the medical examiner," he said to the officer. "That man isn't unconscious. He's dead."

"He can't be dead," I said. "He was alive a few minutes ago."

"I'm sorry, ma'am. Was he your husband?"

"No, he was my professor. How did he die?"

"Cause of death is up to the medical examiner to determine." He walked away.

I turned back to Officer Young. His partner finished up a phone call and approached us. "The ME is on his way. So's homicide."

"Homicide?" The word never lost its impact.

Officer Young said, "Until we know the details of this man's death, this is all routine. You can wait in your car if you like, but I can't let you leave just yet."

"Can I make a phone call?"

"Sure."

The temperature was close to eighty, and coupled with the random heat flashes that came with my age and the swelling in my previously-injured knee, I had to sit. The path of least resistance was the passenger seat of my car, so that was where I went. I closed the door and called Tex again.

"I'm going to be late," I said when he answered. "*Later*."

"Me too. I just sent the two Sues on a call, and I'm not going to leave until I hear how bad it is."

"Was this call to the college?" I asked to confirm what I already knew.

"Night, are you okay?" Tex's voice was tight.

I'd lost count of how many times Tex and I had navigated situations like this. Our relationship complicated everything about his job. "My professor is the victim. He was alive when I called you. There's a patrol cop here with EMTs. The medical examiner is on his way."

"Is there anything you need to tell me before I see the report?"

"My scarf is inside the car."

Tex didn't respond at first. "You were in the car with the professor?" he asked. His voice was still strained, and I pictured him keeping his emotions in check. At a recent physical, the doctors had warned him about the dangers of high blood pressure, but he wrote it off as a side effect of his job. He'd picked up hours at the shooting range, which seemed a volatile way to blow off steam, but in his line of work was probably more common than I knew.

"No. His car was broken into, and the passenger-side door wouldn't stay closed. I gave him my scarf to secure it from the inside. I called you, and when I turned back to him, he was slumped over. I called 911, they told me to check the tailpipe, and that was when I saw something had been jammed inside of it."

"This doesn't sound good."

"It sounds like murder, doesn't it?"

"It doesn't sound like an accident." His voice relaxed. "Stay put. I'll get there as soon as I can."

"No. You have officers on the way. I'll tell you everything tonight."

"Keep a level head and cooperate."

"I gave my statement to Officer Young," I said. "Do you know him?"

"He's Dallas County. Part-time officer. He picked up some of our extra shifts this week."

I temporarily forgot the drama in the parking structure. Recent budget cuts in the police department had forced Tex to cut all full-time positions and run his department on a skeleton staff. He'd hoped to secure funding from some of Dallas's wealthier residents, but they put their money where their police stations were, namely, Park Cities. The divisive budget cuts left many of the smaller community-serving stations in the same predicament as Tex's, and part-time officers started stacking shifts from multiple precincts to make a full-time wage.

"Here comes another police car," I said. "I have to go."

"Call me when you're done."

The police car was followed by a sunset beige SUV. Ling Tsu and Sue Niedermeyer got out of the police car. They were the two female homicide officers at the LPD. At first, they'd each been assigned to different partners, but it turned out their effectiveness went through the roof when they were paired together. They boasted a 99 percent rating on suspect confessions, which the rest of the officers turned into a meme: "You've been Sued." I'd suggested they teach a class.

The driver of the second car was Lloyd. He was the medical examiner for Dallas County. I'd met him for the first time a few months ago and had hoped for purely selfish reasons not to encounter him again for a long time. Longer than four months, for sure.

Lloyd parked his SUV across three parking spaces and got out. He was a lanky man with a shaved head and a goatee that was somewhere between soul patch and Satan. He nodded at the two Sues and completely ignored the patrol cops, but when he saw me, he paused. Lloyd was relatively new to Dallas and wasn't aware of my familiarity with dead bodies. It was possible he was trying to place where he'd seen me before. Cocktail party? Nope. Karaoke bar? Not that either. Coroner's office? Check.

Lloyd and the EMT exchanged brief words. Ling joined them. The EMT gestured to the body resting on the gurney. Lloyd removed the blanket and conducted a quick inspection of Professor Gallagher. His body had been covered by a thick wool blanket. If I didn't already know he was off to a cooler plane, I might have suggested a more seasonable coverup.

Lloyd stood up. "Cause of death appears to be general hypoxia caused by asphyxiation. I'd like to conduct an autopsy to find out more. Look for any clues to indicate he had difficulty breathing."

I stepped forward. "There's something in his tail pipe," I said. The officers turned to me. "I'm a student here. His car was broken into, and the door wouldn't stay shut. I helped him move his files and then gave him my scarf to secure the door. He appeared fine. I turned away to make a phone call, and when I turned back, he was slumped against the wheel."

Lloyd looked inside the car and then straightened up and pointed inside. He said something to Ling. She looked inside the car and said something to Sue, who looked in the car and then stood upright. "You say you gave him your scarf to secure the door?"

"Yes. The door was bent away from the frame, and the scarf was intended to keep it tight. Why are you all focused on my scarf? Isn't the blocked tailpipe the more suspicious thing here?"

"The car should have blown an obstruction out of the tailpipe. In a closed space, with the car idling, sure, carbon monoxide emissions might have seeped into the vehicle and caused suffocation, but if there was a gap between the door frame and the car, fresh air would have offset the danger."

I gulped. "You mean if he hadn't tied the door shut, he might still be alive."

5

LING LEFT THE MEDICAL EXAMINER WITH THE EMT AND STOOD with me. "You couldn't have known," she said. "If that car door swung open while he was driving, it would have caused an accident. It's rush hour. The number of cars on the road is at its peak. He could have caused a major pile-up that endangered many lives."

It was little consolation.

Sue Niedermeyer, the stockier of the two Sues, walked the perimeter of the car. She held her cell phone in front of her and videoed the evidence. I waited a few feet behind her, unsure if she even knew I was there. When she finished, she and Ling exchanged a glance that contained an entire conversation. Ling nodded, and Sue turned to me.

"I assume you gave your statement to one of the officers?"

"Yes," I said. "Officer Young."

"Then you're free to leave. We'll be in touch with any additional questions."

"I can't leave," I said. "Professor Gallagher parked me in."

It was closing in on eight o'clock when I finally returned home. I parked alongside the hedges and used the side entrance. My number-one concern was Rocky, my fluffy caramel and white Shih Tzu who'd been cooped up for most of the day. He sat inside the door and stared up at me with giant apologetic eyes.

I found a pile of poop by the front door. I found an empty box of Peanut Butter Patties under the kitchen table. When I left, that box was full. The deposit Rocky left by the front door was just the beginning.

"We're going out," I said.

I clipped on his leash, grabbed my Nature's Miracle pooper scooper, and left. The sun had set, and the muggy climate had cooled, leaving a wet chill in the air. I doubled back for a thin cardigan and pulled it on while Rocky sniffed the grass. We made it all of three feet before he made deposit number two.

As I engaged Nature's Miracle, a Jeep rumbled down the street. The driver parked behind my Alfa Romeo, and Tex got out.

Whenever I saw Tex, I had a physical reaction. At first, that reaction had been instant animosity. He was roughly my age (after fifty, the lines blurred), physically fit, and aged in a good way. His hair color shifted between dark blond and light brown depending on the season and the sunlight, and his eyes were the blue of faded denim.

In Doris Day's time, Tex would have been referred to as a cad. My first impression was a toxic bachelor with entitlement issues. He'd been overly confident, ordered people around, and treated me as if I knew nothing. I soon learned he was a local homicide detective and the setting for our meet cute was a crime scene.

Occasionally, extenuating circumstances forced one to recalibrate one's first impressions.

Since then, I'd gotten to know him as an investigating officer then as a person. We became friends with an undercurrent of attraction. I denied it vehemently; what self-respecting independent businesswoman dated a man with a loyalty card from the local strip club? But in time, I dropped my preconceived notions and my emotional barriers and saw him for who he was: exciting, reliable, and smart.

"I didn't know you were coming over," I said.

"Shhhh." He strode toward me and wrapped me in an embrace.

The journey to coupledom with Tex was awkward; his bachelor ways had left broken hearts and empty beds scattered all over Dallas. And me? I'd been defiantly single after a life-changing lie inspired me to flee my home state of Pennsylvania for Texas and start a new life with a knee injury. I started Mad for Mod, adopted a puppy, fell for my handyman, and then lost it all (except for the puppy). I wasn't exactly batting a thousand in the relationship department either.

I relaxed into Tex's chest and inhaled the scent of laundry detergent faint on his shirt. Rocky wound his leash around our legs. I leaned away and looked into Tex's ice blue eyes. "Did you talk to Ling or Sue?"

"I talked to Lloyd. The Sues will fill me in tomorrow morning."

"He told you about my scarf."

"You couldn't have known."

I shifted my attention to Rocky, who was in the process of making another deposit dangerously close to my sneaker. I tried to step to the left, but the leash wound around our legs made it impossible. "Untangle," I instructed. Tex took the leash and wound it around my back, behind his, and back to me until we were free. Sadly, I still managed to step in Rocky's mess, and stinky brown poop squished under my sole.

"I'll take Rock around the block," Tex said. He hadn't anticipated the rhyme, and we both laughed. I left him with the leash, ruffled Rocky's fur, and tossed my sneaker in the trash before going back inside.

By the time Tex and Rocky returned, I was surrounded by textbooks. Rocky, happy to be off his leash (and probably a pound lighter), took off up the stairs.

Tex got a beer out of the fridge. "How was your first day of class?"

"Not what I expected."

I lived like I decorated, and just after my fiftieth birthday, I'd completely overhauled my kitchen. It was a study in yellow and white, cheerful to a fault. The last thing I'd done was swap out my existing diner-style dining table with a walnut one that lacked designer mark or provenance. I surrounded it with a set of American of Martinsville walnut and cane high back dining chairs I'd found missing their cushions by a Dumpster in Irving. I remedied that problem with fabric from my vintage stash and foam from Joann Fabrics, and now the buttery-yellow chenille fabric matched perfectly.

Tex dropped into one of the chairs. "C'mon, Night, it's been a long time since I dated a coed." He grinned. "Work with me."

I shook my head in pretend disgust. "My first class was Radical Business Strategy. The professor was like an attack dog. I thought colleges encouraged higher learning after they got your money. He acted like I wasn't good enough to be his student."

"Radical Business Strategy doesn't sound like an entry-level course."

"It's not. It's part of Van Doren's accelerated program. Solid schedule of classes Monday through Friday. I audited entry level courses all last week as a refresher, and they're old hat. This course got me going, and now it's all going to change." I set my pen down.

"Why?"

"I imagine they'll bring in a replacement to teach the rest of the course, but there was something about Gallagher that fired his students up."

Tex set down his beer. "Night, I don't want you going back to that class."

"Oh, for Pete's sake, it's a college that's been operational since 1956. I talked my way into an accelerated five-day course load and I've already paid my tuition in full with money I should have saved for upcoming rent on my empty studio. Besides, the campus is probably going to be swimming with cops now that this happened."

"Why would you think that?"

"Any time there's a murder, you increase police presence in the area as a deterrent. Why would this be any different?"

"We still don't know whether this was murder or a college prank gone wrong. The jammed tailpipe should have caused the car to stall out, not fill the cabin with carbon monoxide. I had my cousin Mickey tow the car to the impound lot, where it's going to sit until we can get an automotive forensic expert to give us a full report of what happened."

"But it's a campus filled with students. You can't ignore the need for heightened police presence."

"That's right, it is a campus, and they have campus police. And frankly, my department is too thin to assign officers to surveil parked cars."

"The campus police will be beefed up, right? A professor is murdered at the college. That's going to make people nervous. They have an obligation to provide a safe environment."

"That safe environment extends to the dorms and the frat parties. Safe environment means something totally different to an eighteen-year-old college student than it does to you."

"You're saying nothing is going to change?"

Tex and I stared at each other. My question became rhetorical by default. Finally, he offered up the same caution as earlier. "Just be careful, Night. We know how Professor Gallagher died, but we still don't know why."

Tex offered to stay the night, but I declined. We both had a full agenda come morning, and I was far from caught up with my coursework. We agreed to check our respective schedules tomorrow after work and try to act like normal people. I often wondered if that was as alien a term to Tex as it was to me.

———

The next morning, I woke early and packed for a morning swim before class. It was blissfully uneventful. After finishing an hour-long set, I showered and changed from my bathing suit to a lavender T-shirt with purple trim and matching purple A-line skirt. I pulled on purple Keds, powdered my face and applied a perky pink lipstick, and left.

When the decorator who lobbied and won the lawsuit against me took possession of my inventory, he dismissed my vast clothing collection. My unique business plan of acquiring estates in full had left me with more vintage clothes than I could wear in ten lifetimes. Instead of fully incorporating the clothes into my closet, I kept them organized by original owner complete with their obituary. It wasn't intentionally morbid; it was my way of honoring the women who first owned the items I loved.

To appropriately get into the spirit of going back to school, I stayed with my education-themed wardrobe choices. Today's outfit first belonged to Gwendolyn Yeary, a kindergarten teacher from Oak Lawn during the civil rights movement. Chasing five-year-olds around a classroom had taken its toll on her clothes, and a few remained unstained by what I liked to imagine was juice. Her estate included a scrapbook filled with newspaper clippings of political speeches and events around town and even a bus ticket to Montgomery, Alabama. She had taught at the school for twelve years, leaving to start a family in the early seventies.

I arrived at the school early enough to drop off my signed paperwork from yesterday. Considering the state of Professor Gallagher, it felt like I was trying to get away with something.

An older woman was behind the counter. She had gray hair cut short and curled professionally. Her shirtdress was a practical choice for her figure. A thin self-belt of matching white cotton was tied around where her waist might have been. She had excellent posture and a take-no-prisoners attitude.

"Hello," I said. "I'm Madison Night. I'm an MBA candidate. Professor Gallagher signed my request form yesterday morning, but I didn't have time to turn it in."

"Radical Business Strategy?" she asked.

"Yes. How did you know?"

"I'm Barbara, the executive assistant to the business

school." She held her hand out and bent it forward several times. "Hand over your paperwork so I can process it," she said.

Barbara was a battleax. Strong, efficient, and no-nonsense. They were the perfect qualities for someone running the admissions office, especially when interacting with students who were in that awkward phase before entering the workforce and discovering there was no such thing as extra credit in the real world. I understood why she maintained her gruff exterior; I just didn't know why she maintained it with me.

I pulled the signed papers out of my backpack and gave them to Barbara. She was acting as though she hadn't heard about what happened. I'd been so busy combing over my textbooks and prepping for today that I hadn't turned on the news, but I couldn't imagine how the school would try to keep something like this to themselves.

"Anything else?" the woman asked.

"No, but do I need to wait for a copy?" I glanced at the clock on the wall. "I have a few minutes before class starts."

"Your class is at seven o'clock tonight."

"Tonight? No, there must be some mistake. Class is at eight o'clock in the morning. I attended it yesterday."

"That was before the professor left us in the lurch. If there's a problem with your schedule, talk to the dean."

6

I HADN'T EXPECTED THE EXECUTIVE ASSISTANT TO MALIGN THE professor so soon after his murder. "What did the professor do?" I asked.

Barbara set down my papers and looked at me over the tops of her reading glasses. "Now, don't go gossiping this around, but Professor Gallagher committed suicide yesterday."

"Suicide?" My surprise at the word trumped my ability to play it cool.

"Shhhh." She patted the air between us to accompany her librarian-worthy shush. "A student found him in his car in the parking structure."

"Who?"

"The police aren't releasing her name. Probably that blonde that's always meeting with him after class."

I didn't tell her she was talking to the blonde in question. "The professor was full of vitality just yesterday morning. It seems hard to believe."

"He was a blustery fellow, that's for sure. Has a whole file of complaints against him. Between you, me, and the display case, the college is better off without him."

Barbara carried my signed forms to the copy machine and opened the lid. A piece of paper lay face-down. Her face scrunched up in consternation. "What's this?" she said to herself.

"I think that belongs to one of my classmates," I said quickly, remembering Eric using the copier. I held my hand out. "I can take it to him."

"Sure," she said. She handed me the flyer and made copies of my application then handed me the originals and filed the copies in a large gray metal cabinet. Her efficiency was a marvel.

I backed away from the desk and read the piece of paper. It was an announcement for Bongo Night at Kanin's, a local after-hours club. The illustrations appeared to have been lifted from vintage men's magazines, equal parts copyright violation and a demonstration of poor taste. I folded the flyer and slid it into my bag.

I called the police department, hoping to catch Tex there. A female voice answered instead.

"Hello," I said cautiously. "This is Madison Night. Is Captain Allen available?"

"Madison! It's Imogene. Long time no chat."

Imogene was a mystery writer who answered the ad for a civilian desk manager, greeted me. Being a volunteer meant she worked as much as she wanted, and being a writer meant she embraced excuses not to actually write.

"How are things at the station?" I asked.

"Quiet," she said. It was an unusual response considering they were investigating a homicide, and I said as much. "Not that kind of quiet. Quiet around here. When I started volunteering, there were cops around. Made my research easy. Now the best conversations I get are between Captain Allen and the police commissioner."

"Are they there now?"

"They just left."

Imogene, in addition to showing up on time and understanding how the archaic telephone transferring and hold system worked, had a near-obsessive interest in police matters. Tex once told me she asked more questions than a conspiracy theorist in a room filled with politicians. Her book-in-progress was multi-layered thanks, in part, to what she picked up from volunteering at the precinct. We were all a little afraid she might get it published.

"If you want, I can transfer you to his cell."

"Sure," I said. I thanked her and wished her luck with her research, and then waited while she put me on hold. A few seconds later, Tex answered. "It's me," I said. "Not an emergency." It wasn't a common greeting but considering his role as the captain of the police and my role as finder of dead bodies, it worked for us.

"Hey, Night. How's my favorite college student?"

"A little overtaxed, if you want the truth. The college moved my eight o'clock class to seven tonight, so I'm going to have to cancel dinner."

"Isn't that the class Gallagher taught?"

"Yes."

"What's it called again?"

"Radical Business Strategy."

"Right. Who's going to teach it now?"

"I don't know. The admissions desk receptionist said he committed suicide. Did Lloyd change the cause of death?"

"Haven't heard from Lloyd yet today, but there's no reason

to think the college would know something we don't. Probably just gossip nobody wants to correct."

"I almost corrected her," I said. "It felt wrong to hear her imply he inconvenienced the college by dying."

Tex was quiet for longer than seemed natural. "Are you still there?" I asked.

"Sorry. Investors are calling. See you tonight." He disconnected.

With newfound time on my schedule, I bought a cup of coffee at the School Pride kiosk and killed time observing photos in the display case. One grouping caught my attention. It was a compilation of graduates who'd gone on to run successful business in Dallas. The third picture from the right on the second row was someone who'd been in and out of my life for years. Donna Nast, CEO and owner of Big Bro Security.

Donna, or Nasty, as I (and many people who'd had the pleasure of interacting with her) sometimes called her, was a former police officer turned independent business owner who'd helped me out enough times that I no longer thought of her as my nemesis.

Frenemy was a better term.

It came as no surprise that Nasty had graduated from Van Doren College. Nasty was self-interested in a way that would have made Ayn Rand proud. She left the police force after recognizing she would never be—and didn't want to be—part of the boy's club culture that existed at the time. She opened Big Bro Security and focused on the private sector. Her efforts were rewarded with exponential growth, a word-of-mouth reputation, and a demand that far surpassed her supply. She'd invested in my business when I had one, not because she wanted to help but because, at the time, it was a sound investment. I guess there was a time when I *was* good on paper.

Since then, Nasty's company expanded from business security to private home security. She'd also had a baby sired by one of the most successful architects in the area. He was in his late seventies. One could have made a case that Nasty's focus on wealth appropriation bordered on pathological, but in this case, I knew better. Despite the fifty-year gap in their ages, they were two peas in a pod.

Before I thought twice about it, I called her. We weren't in the habit of calling each other for anything other than matters of importance, so I was surprised when she answered.

"What's up, Madison?"

"Hello to you too," I said.

"I finally got Huxley to sleep. If the phone wakes him, I'm in for another hour of 'Rock-A-Bye Baby.'"

"You could turn your ringer off."

"I'm waiting for a call." She waited a beat and then added, "Not yours."

Donna Nast was everybody's favorite person to hate—until they got to know her. And she didn't let a lot of people know her. She was twenty-nine, sexy, independent, and smart. She didn't make a decision without her endgame in mind, and that had, at times, both simplified and complicated my life.

"Did you attend Van Doren College?"

"That was where I got my MBA. Why?"

"A professor from the business school died yesterday. Gallagher. Did you have him?"

"No." There was a quick beat of silence, and then, "He was murdered?"

"I said died. I didn't say murder."

"Madison, there's no way you would know about this unless Tex told you, Tex wouldn't know about it unless it was a police matter. I thought you understood we don't do the whole hello/how-are-you routine."

"I'm enrolled at Van Doren. I was with the professor when he died. The story around the college is that he committed suicide, but I don't think that was what happened. I saw your picture in the display case at the Canfield Building and called you."

"When's your next class?"

"Not until eleven."

"Go to the library and don't leave until I get there. We need to talk."

———

THE MAIN CAMPUS of Van Doren College was laid out in a giant pentagon. The Canfield Building resided outside the original arrangement of buildings. The library was on the opposite side sandwiched between the homes of Arts and of Sciences.

Early birds were in the quad today. The few students I passed didn't seem to notice me. The campus was quiet, and the sound of birds chirping dominated the air. Rocky would love it here. I wondered how the faculty would view a peppy Shih Tzu attending one of their classes.

I entered the library and claimed a seat at a large wooden table by the front door. I couldn't stop thinking about Professor Gallagher. I remembered again about how he'd used Mad for Mod as his case study and encouraged the room to determine my possible course of action. Instead of working on any of my homework assignments, I opened a notebook to a blank page and filled it with ideas. After my ideas, I wrote: *Expand. Go Big. Invest. Double Down,* and in block letters after that, I wrote: *TAKE RISKS.*

Gallagher had called them power words, but they lacked power to me. They represented antiquated Gordon Gekko-esque philosophies still embraced by men who smoked cigars in clubs with leather chairs. I wore preowned dresses and hats that looked like flowerpots, and my favorite chair was named after a womb—the polar opposite of what you'd find in a men's club. I lacked the killer instincts required to conduct business in a ruthless manner. And until recently, it had worked out for me.

I didn't need to reinvent myself, I just needed to go back to my roots and do things the way I'd always done them. It was like I'd told the class: there were extenuating circumstances. The client knew it. I knew it. Even the other decorator knew it.

I'd made a careless mistake by publicly taking credit for a job I hadn't designed. It had happened in the week after Doris Day died, and even though the actress was ninety-seven at the time, her death hit me hard. I didn't know her, but she'd been a part of my life for as long as I could remember.

We shared a birthday. My parents used to buy me one of her movies each year on April third, and we'd sit together around a big bowl of popcorn and celebrate. It was how I honed my eye for mid-century design. It was why I decided to become a decorator. And when my parents were killed in a car crash, it was Doris Day's brand of cheerful resilience I channeled. When she died, the other shoe from my parents' death dropped too, and I'd been leveled. Nobody would have been thinking straight.

When I had a chance to talk to the decorator on the other

side of the lawsuit, he understood. The case had gotten too far into the courts by then, so when the ruling went in his direction, he arranged for me to keep my business name and decorating license. My original business plan had been successful for the past ten years. Why change now?

I didn't need to take risks. All I needed was capital so I could fill my showroom with inventory and book new clients. Professor Gallagher was the shock jock of business teachers, and he needed to make my problem seem big so he could use them for his lecture. But maybe he and the banks had blown my problems out of proportion.

I flipped to a new page in my notebook and started a list of clients I could call for referrals. Everything would be fine. School might be an inconvenience, but I might not even need the degree to show the banks they were wrong.

A shadow fell across my notebook, and I looked over my shoulder to see Donna Nasty reading my new business plan with a baby strapped to her chest.

"I hate to tell you, Madison, but you're going to need more than client referrals to dig your way out of this one."

7

I slapped my notebook closed. "That was private," I said to Nasty.

"I'm not interested in a list of people who hired you to install Sputnik lamps in their dining rooms," she said. She kept her hand on her baby's back and swayed ever so slightly. She'd given birth two months ago, and in typical Nasty fashion, had rebounded with ease. Her long copper and bronze streaked hair was pulled back into a low ponytail, and she wore her usual white ribbed tank top and jeans. Huxley had his head turned to the side of her ample breasts. He wore a light blue knit hat and a matching onesie, and even though I'd never regretted my decision not to have children, I was tempted to reach out and clasp his little foot.

If I weren't a little afraid of Mamma Bear, I might have followed through with the impulse.

"What was that?" she asked, pointing at my notebook.

Nasty had played a role in the lawsuit's outcome, but we hadn't talked much about the ruling thanks to Huxley's arrival and subsequent demands on her attention. She'd received a surge of public praise after turning over evidence that led to a murderer's conviction, and shortly thereafter, went into labor. I hadn't seen her since.

"Hi, Donna," I said.

"Yeah. Hi. What was that?" she asked. Motherhood had softened her. Not!

"Notes for one of my business classes."

"They want you to make a list of people who have nothing to do with your current dilemma?"

"If you saw the list, then why are you asking me what it is?"

"Because I know you're too smart to sit around longing for the past even if your wardrobe indicates otherwise."

"I want my business back. I'm brainstorming how to do that."

She glanced around the library. "We can't talk in here. Come with me." She turned around and walked away. I jammed my notebook into my backpack and followed about twenty feet behind. I caught up to her in front of the Arts Building. "Walk and talk," she said. "Tell me about Professor Gallagher."

"I first met him two days ago in his office. The semester already started, so I had to talk my way in. He made no secret of the fact that he didn't think I would last."

"But he signed your late admittance requisition?"

"Yes."

"Huh."

I'd had enough conversations with Nasty to know she processed information faster than Fortran. Her occasional interjections in our conversation weren't for me. She took in data and hit her mental enter key to compute. Occasionally she'd ask a direct question to clarify something, which I likened to a circular reference. Once I started imagining Nasty as a computer program, we got along a lot better.

"Between my meeting with him and class, he must have looked me up, because he used my circumstances as a case study for discussion. At first, I thought he wanted to humiliate me, but it might have been to see how I responded to the material."

"Probably a little of both. You don't look like you can take it. If you were going to drop out, it would save everybody's time if you did it sooner rather than later."

"Why does everybody think I'm incapable of operating like a businessperson?"

"Have you looked in the mirror lately?"

"You don't have to shop at Brooks Brothers to be in business."

"Yes, but if you want the banks to see you as a good risk, it doesn't hurt to look the part."

It had to have been a guess. There was no way she could have known about my day of rejection and my trouble securing a start-over loan. But her comment hit too close to home, and I got defensive. "I did it once, I can do it again."

"I'm sure you can. How did you do it the first time?"

"I put everything I had into an apartment building and rented it out. I used the income from my tenants to fund my business. In time, the business was doing well, so I sold the apartment building."

"Which you regretted, because you bought it back."

"That wasn't regret. I needed a property to renovate for a county-wide competition. You know this. You were one of my investors."

"When you first met me, did you ever expect me to invest in your business?"

"No."

"But I did. Do you know why?"

"You thought I was good on paper?"

"You're crap on paper. But you have passion for what you do, and people respond to passion." She rubbed her hand up and down Huxley's back. "If I had to guess, I'd say you didn't respond well to the professor using your company as a case study in class."

I thought back to the feeling I'd had when Gallagher first described my situation. "He should have asked me if it was okay first."

Nasty shook her head. "What's the name of your course?"

"Radical Business Strategy."

"What gave you the impression he was going to do anything according to a code of consideration?"

I shrugged. "I just thought, you know, this is a college. The professors should want their students to learn, not to scare them off."

"The two aren't mutually exclusive."

Sometimes I hated talking to Nasty. It was easier when I wrote her off as being one of Tex's former girlfriends, but so much had happened since then that in her words, they were a blip on the radar.

I didn't answer, mostly because I was tired of her making me think. Her question hung in the air until Huxley woke up and burped. Nasty pulled out a green towel with pictures of dollar bills on it (kidding!) and dabbed his mouth. He blew a spit bubble and then closed his eyes and laid his head against her bosom. He wriggled in his harness and then fell back to sleep.

I secretly hoped he kept her up at night.

"Tell me what happened with Gallagher in the parking structure," she said.

Happy the subject had shifted, I told her how I'd caught up with the professor in Lot B, how his car had been broken into, how I gave him my scarf to secure the passenger-side door, and how he slumped over the wheel shortly thereafter. I described the blockage in his tailpipe and the medical examiner's stated cause of death: general hypoxia caused by asphyxiation. I ended with the rumor that the professor had committed suicide.

"What did Tex say about it?" she asked.

"Nothing. Not nothing. He didn't have much to tell. He said his cousin towed the car to the police impound lot where it'll wait until he can get a forensic automotive expert to look at it."

"Forensic automotive is a rare field. It's probably going to take longer than Tex wants to find someone qualified."

"Will that matter? A car is a car."

Nasty shrugged. "This guy didn't commit suicide," she said.

"I don't think so either, but—"

She cut me off. "It's not a theory. It's a fact. When he started the car, the rag would have been blown out of the tailpipe or the car would have stalled."

"But that's not what happened. The car started and ran. I was behind it. There was no exhaust. One of the homicide detectives said if the passenger-side door hadn't been tied shut, enough fresh air would have gotten in to keep him alive."

"Who took the call?"

"The two Sues," I said. Nasty's forehead creased. "Ling Tsu and Sue Niedermeyer. They're new to the Lakewood PD."

"Looks like diversity has found the police department."

"They're good. Best confession rate in the state. Tex said

other police departments have asked him to send them to train their squads."

"Sounds like a different world since I left." She rested her hands on Huxley's back and ran them up and down his little spine. I saw a flicker of something cross her face. It flashed across her features so quickly I didn't have time to identify the emotion.

"I'd say there are two possibilities here. One, someone tampered with the professor's tailpipe and rerouted the exhaust into the cabin, or two, someone poisoned him ahead of time and the vandalism to his car caused his pulse to speed up and the poison to absorb faster. Either way, we're not looking at suicide. We're looking at murder."

8

No matter how I felt about Nasty, it was impressive to watch her work. In a matter of minutes, receiving a second-hand account of the crime scene, she had a working theory that sounded legit. I was dating the captain of the police department, and all I had was this lousy T-shirt.

"What should we do?" I asked her.

"I'm not going to do anything. Correction. I'm taking Huxley to his father's house and then going to the office to work on a proposal. You, most likely, are going to your next class unless you've already decided to let the professor be right by dropping out."

"I'm not dropping out."

"Then I guess we know what we're doing next."

I packed up my books. We walked side by side, the conversation lapsing into silence. The time I spent in the library, coupled with the conversation with Nasty, had spread beyond the time I would have normally been in my eight o'clock class. The formerly empty quad was filled with students headed between buildings and clusters idled by the entrances. I checked my watch, a vintage Seiko, and saw I had three minutes to return to Canfield for my foundational course. It was in a lecture hall, and I'd go undetected if I slipped in through a back door, but I didn't want to get into the habit of being late.

"I have to run," I said. "Decision Making for the Business Leader starts at eleven."

"Why are you doing this?" Nasty asked. "Business school. Why now?"

"Because I have the time." I knew it was a lie. Nasty probably knew it was a lie too. I sighed. "Every bank I applied to turned down my loan application. None of them think I have a solid business plan. It's like going to a foreign country. I can probably get by, but it might be easier if I learn the language."

She raised one (perfectly tweezed) eyebrow and tipped her head toward the Canfield Building. "Van Doren is a good school. I hope it works out for you."

She turned her back on me and walked away.

***

DECISION MAKING for the Business Leader was followed by Ethics, Accounting, and finally Statistics, which ended at six thirty. My brain was numb from classroom learning. I'd planned my course load to hit the ground running with my most challenging course first thing in the morning, and now, it was the cap to my day. While most people were unwinding with a cocktail, I was summoning the last remaining vestiges of focus within me.

My Statistics course was in the same room as Radical

Business Strategy, so I remained in the room. "RISK" was still on the chalkboard. I'd stared at the word through the entire previous lecture. I'd taken bigger risks starting my business than most people took in a lifetime. Without thinking, I picked up a thick piece of blue chalk and drew a line through the word and then again and again and again. Before I realized what I had done, I'd obliterated what was possibly the last lesson Professor Gallagher had written.

"Well, I'll be. Who did that?" asked a deep male voice.

With the incriminating piece of chalk in my hand, I turned around. An older man in a khaki suit, white shirt, and cowboy boots stood behind me. I'd been so involved in my serial-killer graffiti that I hadn't heard him enter. I balled my fist up around the chalk.

"Someone who isn't a fan of risk," the man added. He looked around the empty classroom and then back at me. "Madison Night, correct?"

"Yes," I said.

"I'm the dean of the business school. Hugo Wallace." He held out his hand.

I slipped my fists into the pockets of my purple skirt and released the chalk then pulled my hand out and shook his. "My last class was in this room, so I didn't have far to walk." I smiled. "I was going to come see you tomorrow. I had specifically wanted to take this course in the morning, and I built the rest of my schedule around it."

"Let's take things one step at a time. This was Professor Gallagher's brainchild, and without him here to teach it, we're not sure how to proceed. We may pull it from the curriculum."

"But the admissions receptionist told me it was moved to a night timeslot. That's why I'm here." I glanced at the clock.

"There are twenty other students taking this course. It's too late for them to find other 400-level courses to fill the hole in their schedules, and that might keep people from graduating."

"When you spoke to Barbara this morning, the plan had been to find a professor to stand in and complete the course. Finding a replacement isn't the problem. The problem is with the material."

I couldn't believe what I heard. All across the country, institutions of higher learning were being criticized for classes deemed controversial, but here at Van Doren, they were going to play it safe.

"This is one of the most talked-about classes in your business program," I said.

"After what happened yesterday, I took the liberty of going through the professor's syllabus," Hugo said. "Professor Gallagher's ideas were dangerous. He's had a slew of complaints over the years, two threatening legal action. The board of education warned him…" The dean stopped talking mid-sentence. "It's a shame what happened, but in some ways it's a blessing in disguise. Van Doren College doesn't need his brand of controversy."

"But isn't that the foundation of learning? Healthy discussion, new viewpoints? Make people consider information even when they disagree with it?"

"It seems I'm in agreement with our graffiti artist," he said, motioning toward the chalkboard. "The board is having an emergency meeting later tonight where we'll vote on a decision, but the writing appears to be on the wall—er, the chalkboard." He seemed pleased with his joke and glanced at me to gauge my response. I was too distracted to care about witticisms.

Everything I'd studied earlier that day had been rote.

Accounting taught how to balance a profit and loss statement. Statistics taught the likelihood of a return on investments. Ethics was a required course for everyone at Van Doren regardless of their major, and Decision Making for the Business Leader was something I'd been doing by osmosis for years.

And here was a subject that taught people to think differently. To challenge the status quo. As much as I resisted the need to do so, I couldn't deny how riled up I'd gotten in yesterday's class. Even the professor had commented on it: whether it was my anger toward him or my defense of my business, I'd landed on the right words to frame what I needed to do to rebound. Radical Business Strategy was the best course the college offered, and the dean was going to cancel it.

"You just said you had a long day of classes," Hugo said. "If we cancel this course, your evenings will be free. Every student needs a social life." He winked.

Oh, please. I packed up my backpack. "Are you leaving too?" I asked the dean.

"No, I'm going to stay behind in case there are any other students who didn't get the message."

As if on cue, Eric dashed into the classroom. His backpack was slung over the shoulder of his wrinkled blue checkered shirt and his bowtie was askew. He seemed surprised at finding an empty room with just the dean and me and stopped suddenly. His backpack fell off his shoulder and landed in one of the many vacant seats.

"Where is everybody?" he asked. He looked back and forth between mine and the dean's faces. He was out of breath, and I imagined he'd had similar scheduling complications as I had when he learned our course was being moved.

"Class has been canceled for today," I said. I wasn't willing to accept the board of education would agree with the dean so easily and added the "for today" as a challenge to see if he'd contradict me.

"You mean I raced over here for nothing?" He picked his backpack up and slung it over both shoulders. "Tell the admissions office to do a better job of communicating to the student body," he said to the dean. "The student body who *pays tuition.*" He shook his head, disgusted by the scheduling snafu, and left with as much bluster as he'd arrived.

The dean was unfazed. "I'm going to have to lock the classroom for the night." He held his arm out, palm forward, as if ushering me toward the door. "Once the board decides how to proceed, you'll be notified."

I walked into the hallway and Hugo followed. "Good night, Madison." He stood in the doorway with the door mostly closed behind him. I said goodnight and left. When I reached the end of the hallway, I turned back around. The door to room 102 was closed, but the light was still on. The dean was nowhere to be seen.

I'd been humiliated when Gallagher used Mad for Mod as his case study in class yesterday, but the idea that I wasn't able to return to that very course now angered me.

If anger was the controversy the college wanted to avoid, they were short-changing their students on the promised education. Sometimes we had to be uncomfortable to learn the lessons that propelled us forward. But the dean had mentioned lawsuits before he caught himself. Someone had a beef with the now-deceased professor, and that didn't seem to be public knowledge.

A part of me knew I needed a kick in the pants. I was back to square one. But in terms of the suspect pool, the field had widened—or it would when I gave this new information to Tex.

9

———

IT WAS A LITTLE AFTER EIGHT BY THE TIME I GOT HOME. THE sun had set, and twilight transitioned to night. Rocky paced back and forth on the other side of the door while I unlocked it. Perhaps if I'd taken him with me to the banks, my entire life would be different. Sometimes I undervalued the effect a rambunctious Shih Tzu had on the public at large.

Rocky yipped a couple of times in rapid succession and hopped up on his hind legs. I ruffled the fur on his head. He snorted his delight at having company. I dropped my backpack and keys onto the table, threw out the stick of chalk from my pocket, and took Rocky outside. He trotted to the end of the concrete and then charged through the yard to the property next door. It was dark, and I feared the worst.

"Rocky!" I called. I ran after him. The grass was cool against my ankles. The temperature had dropped into the high sixties, and I was dressed for temperatures twenty degrees hotter. I found Rocky and a gray striped cat having a stare-off on the other side of the building next door.

"Hello," I said to the cat.

"Hello," said a male voice.

I looked around, not willing to accept the *Alice in Wonderland* moment, and recognized Dennis O'Hara, the realtor who had helped put me into my house, standing under the porch light of the building.

"Dennis," I said, relieved. "For a moment, I thought the Cheshire Cat had relatives."

"Madison," Dennis said casually. "I was hoping to run into you today. How's Thelma Johnson's house?"

A few years ago, a client who had inherited his mother's house gave it to me for the low price of the unpaid annual taxes. I'd bought out his mother's estate when she passed away, which had led to a murder investigation, a conspiracy regarding a Doris Day movie, and a major motion picture due to be released next year, all of which led to a fair amount of notoriety around town and a temporary boost to my business —before my more recent fall from grace.

"Thelma Johnson's house is the one constant in my life," I said. Honestly, if everything else fell into place as easily as the house had, I'd be sitting pretty. I lured Rocky back to my side. The cat sat under a bush by the side of the building and watched him. I glanced from the building to my kitchen windows and wondered if Rocky and the cat had a flirtation going.

Dennis turned away from the door and joined me out front. "You rent a studio on Greenville Avenue, don't you?"

For now. "Yes," I said.

"Have you ever considered something more permanent?"

"What do you have in mind?"

He pointed at the building. "It used to belong to Sam Johnson, Thelma's husband, but she sold it after he died. It's zoned for commercial use. It's not functional for a living space, but with you next door, it could be a good business investment. Too small to use for storage, but you'd build equity. If you ever wanted to move, having this property could add to the value of yours."

I felt the same tingle I'd felt in class. "Can I see the inside?" I asked.

"Not tonight. I wrote down the wrong lockbox code. I have a full day tomorrow, but I'm free on Friday. The owner is looking to unload the building, so if you're interested, I can get you a good price and push things through quickly."

I considered my recent banking woes. "Financing might be a problem," I said.

Dennis shushed my concerns. "That's easy. We take out a home equity loan and invest it here. The banks love transactions like this. They know you're good for the money because you don't want to lose your house, and this additional property makes more sense for you than if it were sitting on the market. Everybody wins."

Everybody except me if I couldn't make the payments.

I made plans to call Dennis and arrange to see the property and then carried Rocky home. The cat kept its eyes on Rocky (and vice versa). Forget flirtation; this had all the earmarks of a grudge match.

It was earlier than it would have been if class had indeed taken place at night but later than usual. Between that and my early-morning swim, I was tired. Most days, I was in bed by nine thirty. The life of a coed indeed!

I unpacked my textbooks and glanced at the required reading, but my mind wasn't engaged. Page after page of foundational business classes told me, in uninspired language, the same lessons I'd learned through experience. I flipped through my notebook and found the page with my ideas and the power words I'd used when Gallagher had baited me: *Expand. Go Big. Double Down. Take Risks.*

Every time I looked at those words, I felt the way I felt in class. Excited. Like something big, something new, was right around the corner. And in this case, it was. Not quite around the corner but next door.

I stood from the table and stared out my kitchen window at the vacant property. It had been for sale for months, and aside from registering the For Sale sign out front, I hadn't thought twice about it. But now, things were different.

I'd been paying rent on an empty studio on Greenville Avenue for the past few months, and those checks had been written first with denial then anger toward the decorator who sued me, the client whose job I had completed, and myself for letting it happen. I'd tried bargaining with the universe: send me a sign that everything will work out, and I'll start putting smiley faces on my checks.

I'd been rewarded with a rusted-out base of a Warren Platner metal rod coffee table that I found next to a dumpster. Like everything else these days, the base required major TLC to bring it back to life. Without the capital to have the work done, it sat in my storage locker behind my studio where it waited for me to get my act together while probably rusting further. The universe may have sent me a sign, but the fine print said things weren't going to be easy.

After bargaining with the universe, I fell into a pit of depression that lasted an embarrassing two weeks. I lied about it to everyone but stopped returning calls of friends and skipped out on a week of swimming. Tex had gone out of town for a recruiting trip, and I spent the time eating Special K cereal three meals a day. By the time he returned, I'd accepted my circumstances. I'd also lost two inches from my waist.

I couldn't say whether it was the immediate effects of business school or the gradual realization that I controlled my future, but the fog had lifted from the crossroads at which I now stood. My problem since the lawsuit had been thinking too small.

All of that was about to change.

1 O

WHEN TEX SHOWED UP AT ELEVEN THIRTY, I WAS SURPRISED TO
see how much time had passed. He, conversely, was surprised
to find me awake.

"Your light was on," he said. "I thought you'd be in bed."

"If you thought I'd be in bed, then why did you come
over?"

He grinned lasciviously. "Pass up an opportunity to sleep
with a college student? I thought that ship had sailed."

"Knowing you, it hasn't been as long as you think."

"I wouldn't trade you for all of them combined." He
reached his hand out and pulled me out of my chair.

We kissed hello. I could see the same exhaustion on Tex's
face that I felt. For completely different reasons, we were
consumed with issues of money and burning the candle at
both ends. We were also both aware that what we'd found
with each other defied logic. Tex could still push my buttons
and I his, but in the end, we were lucky.

The hello kiss turned into a hello trip to the bedroom,

which was edited for brevity. Forty minutes later, we fell asleep under yellow cotton sheets trimmed in daisies, both of our troubles temporarily forgotten.

MY INTERNAL ALARM clock woke me at five. I was alone. It took a moment to remember Tex had been there, and the pile of shoes and socks by the side of the bed confirmed he still was. I got up, pulled on a yellow velvet housecoat with large pink and white flowers appliqued on it, pushed my feet into pink leather Jacques Levine slippers, and went downstairs. Tex was at my kitchen table, flipping through my notebook.

"What's all this?" he asked.

I reached in front of him and closed my notebook. "Homework," I said. It was a white lie that might have been beige. I pulled the books toward me. "I didn't realize I left such a mess down here. Let me get this stuff out of your way."

He grabbed my wrist. "Night."

"Captain Allen."

"I'm not thrilled about you going to that college."

"Yes, and I'm not thrilled about you wandering the streets of Dallas with a loaded gun, but these are the choices we made." I pulled my arm away from him and filled a mug with fresh coffee. When I returned to the table, I sat in a chair opposite him and let the coffee cool for a moment before taking a sip. "You should be happy that I'm at that college. I hear things."

"Like what?"

"Like the college thinks Professor Gallagher's syllabus is controversial." I pulled my mug toward me and took a tentative sip. It was stronger than I usually made it, but I was out of milk, so I powered through. "The dean of the business school said they're still deciding what to do about his syllabus."

"Gallagher was a fraud," Tex said. He leaned back and threaded his fingers behind his head. "I did a deep dive into his background, and his degrees and recommendations are bunk. His book was published by a vanity press. The last school he worked for fired him for accusations of sexual harassment from four different students. He may have propped himself up as a good guy at Van Doren, but in a previous life he was least likely to succeed." He pulled his left arm away from his head, glanced at his tank watch, and then resumed his position. "You usually have a solid bullshit meter. You didn't see any of this?"

"I didn't feel immediate affection for the man, but I attended exactly one of his classes, so I thought I'd give him the benefit of the doubt."

"Drop the Gallagher class," he said. "Find another 400-level course instead. You don't need to be involved in another investigation right now." I studied his clear blue eyes, looking for something to rally against, but all I saw was concern (and disappointment after he glanced down at my housecoat and concluded he wasn't going to get a peek at the goods).

He was right. I didn't need to get involved in another homicide investigation, not now when all my energy needed to go into rebuilding my company. I cut my eyes to the pile of notebooks and textbooks on the table. Had Tex seen my plans? Did he know I'd turned the proverbial corner?

"You're probably right," I said, giving in too soon. "The dean said the college hadn't determined how they were handling Gallagher's course, but I'm sure they can suggest an alternative."

Tex's eyes narrowed almost imperceptibly. I kept mine wide. I had the uncanny feeling we were both hiding something.

After eggs, toast, and coffee with Tex, I dressed in a vintage Lacoste shirt and baggy Bermuda shorts, argyle knee socks, and penny loafers. I said goodbye to Rocky and headed for campus. If I could convince the dean to let me transfer into another eight o'clock course, my life could go back to normal. Ish.

I parked in the same lot, took the same path, and ended up at the same place as I had the morning I talked my way into Professor Gallagher's class. Again, the campus was quiet. The temperature was in the seventies, though seventy degrees in Dallas was bad enough. Humidity clung to the air, testing the strength of my deodorant.

I entered Canfield. I'd expected to find Barbara behind the counter, but she wasn't there. I found Ansel Benedict, the theatrical professor, instead.

"Good morning," he said. He pointed at me and moved his finger around. "You're an early bird. Have you gotten any worms?"

I smiled. "Not yet. Do you know if Dean Wallace is around? I need to talk to him about one of my courses."

"Are you still on the Radical Business Strategy kick?" he asked. He scooped tiny mounds of tobacco into his pipe and then packed the tobacco with the back of his little spoon. "I've gone ten rounds with Gallagher. We shared a classroom wall, and it got so bad, I had mine soundproofed." He leaned forward and said, conspiratorially, "I've heard the lectures. Why anyone would want to study that material is beyond me." He fluttered his hand in the air.

Before I had a chance to reply, the door at the back of the

business office opened, and Barbara entered. Today she wore a yellow shirtdress. I pictured her shopping for the school year, finding a style that worked, and buying it in bulk.

"Hello, Barbara," Ansel said. He turned to me. "Good-bye, Eliza." He made a slight bow toward us both and waved his pipe in the air and then exited through the door at the back of the office.

"He hasn't cast you as a character?" I asked.

"I put a stop to that nonsense immediately. He can call me Barbara like the rest of the school does." She shook her head at the memory and sorted a stack of mail into cubbies that were mounted on the wall. When she finished, she turned to me. "Now, what can I help you with today?"

"Dean Wallace said Radical Business Strategy class might be canceled, and I wanted to find out what other courses are in the eight a.m. slot."

"None, I imagine, but you're in luck. It's too late for the college to add a new course to the curriculum, so Radical Business Strategy remains a viable option."

I was oddly pleased. "Will it return to the original time?"

"No. There was no one available to teach it. The dean is stepping in to fill the spot, but the only available time on his schedule is at night." She glanced at her calendar. "We've already had one withdrawal, but the dean was able to fill the spot from the waitlist."

This was the second time information regarding my class appeared to have been disseminated to the class without my knowledge. "Is there a distro list or an email chain where I can get these updates? It seems if I don't stop by this desk and ask about my classes, I'd be perpetually in the dark."

She tipped her face down and peered at me over her

reading glasses. "You did update your student profile to include this course, didn't you?"

"I forgot," I admitted. "I met with Professor Gallagher on Monday. He signed off on my paperwork and told me to be in class on Tuesday."

"Update your student profile. All updates and course materials are sent through the portal."

I thanked her and left the building.

Somewhere buried in my bag was an orientation packet. Late enrollment had meant jumping into the deep end to get caught up, and that meant things like orientation could wait until later, or so I'd thought. Now I wondered what else I'd missed.

I spent the next couple hours in the library updating my profile and downloading coursework. I saved it all to a flash drive so I could read it more thoroughly when I got home. Already I could tell it was going to be another late night.

By the time seven o'clock rolled around, my full day of catch-up coursework had left me glazed over. It was one thing to balance a budget for your own business but another to spend hours working through business scenarios in a textbook. I would have killed for a decorating class in the middle of it all just to cleanse my palette for learning.

My blood sugar was low, and I had just enough time for a candy bar. I left the classroom with the others and bought a Payday, this being business school and all. The hallway was empty, so I tore into it and ate like no one was watching, wiped my mouth, and headed back.

The classroom door was open, and Faye was in the hallway with a student who hadn't been in class before. He wore a Van Doren T-shirt, jeans, and sneakers, an outfit that made him blend in with just about everybody on campus.

But he didn't blend in. He stood out like a sore thumb. Because despite his attempt to look like everybody else, there was no way to hide his identity from me.

The new student was Tex.

11

TEX SPOTTED ME A MOMENT AFTER I SPOTTED HIM. TO HIS
credit, he lost all interest in Faye. He excused himself, but
instead of coming over to me, he went inside the classroom
and sat down at a desk in the back. Aside from our initial eye
contact, he pretended not to notice me.

"He's cute, right?" Faye said, joining me by the door.
"That's the good thing about night classes. Older men."

"Who is he?" I asked.

"New student. His name is Rex. Rexford Allen. Sounds
wealthy, don't you think? Old Dallas money. He said he's
poised to take over the family business. Tuna, I think. Maybe
it was herring. Something fishy."

She was right about that!

Hugo entered the classroom. "Good evening, students.
Please take your seats. We're about to get started." He turned
to Faye and me. Faye's thumbs were busy tapping away on her
phone screen. "Faye, no cell phones in class."

"Sorry, Dean Wallace," Faye said. Dean looked at me, and I
smiled.

"Madison, I'm happy to see you made it. Did you update your student profile?"

"Yes."

"Oh, good. Barbara said there was a problem with it." He paused and looked across the room at Tex. "Mr. Allen, did Barbara advise you to complete your student profile?"

Tex had the good sense to look confused.

"After class, meet with Ms. Night. She can tell you what you've missed."

Tex shifted his attention from the dean to me for a fraction of a second. I considered sticking out my tongue and crossing my eyes, but, showing great restraint, I did not.

Being creatures of habit, my classmates chose the same seats they'd occupied previously. I forgot the one class session I'd attended had been two weeks into the semester for them; I was as much of a newbie as Tex. The last remaining seat was the one in the front row, directly in the line of fire of the dean. With no other options, I claimed it.

Faye had ignored the instruction of the dean and fixed her attention on her phone. She scrolled slowly, seeming not to notice class was about to start.

Hugo stood next to the desk. "Before we get into the coursework, I have an announcement. Van Doren is saddened by the passing of Professor Gallagher. The college will suspend classes on Monday in his honor. There is no formal memorial, but if anyone chooses to plan one, please leave the information with Barbara at the admissions desk." He stopped talking and studied the faces of the students in class. "Would anyone like to talk about what happened? Does anybody have anything they'd like to say about Professor Gallagher?"

I hadn't expected the dean to talk about the deceased professor, but it made good sense for the college to approach the subject head-on. Still, I got the feeling it was an act for our benefit. The caring dean, stepping in to oversee the stressed-out business students left behind by their loyal leader?

"He was a fraud," Eric muttered. The attention shifted to him, and he looked at the dean. "He tells us to take risks, and then he cops out by committing suicide."

"He didn't kill himself," Faye protested. "Someone tampered with his car."

The color drained from Eric's face. He sat in the middle of the room, in the sightline between Tex and me. I looked past him to Tex, who caught my eye. His gaze was cold and unemotional. It was his cop face, the unreadable one, but if I had to guess, I'd say it communicated something about him telling me to drop this class and me not doing so.

I twisted around to face Faye. "Where did you hear that?"

"It's all over the local news," she said. She held up her phone, but the screen had gone into sleep mode and was dark.

"No phones in class," Hugo repeated.

"I just wanted to show Madison the news story."

"Faye, I'm not going to tell you again. Madison is capable of looking it up when we're done."

Faye put her phone away and looked at me apologetically. "It's all over the news," she said again.

"I still say he's a fraud," Eric said. (We seemed to have been caught in a loop of people repeating themselves.) "What business did Gallagher run? Why are we supposed to pay attention to what he teaches when he doesn't have any success of his own?" He scowled. "Madison, you didn't believe anything he said about you, did you?"

I hadn't expected to be called out so specifically, and I froze.

The dean answered in my place. "Thank you, Eric, for

bringing the discussion back to business. I checked the notes from your last class, and it seems you had a heated discussion about Madison Night's unique business situation. Madison, why don't you recap for us? We have at least two people here who missed class, and speaking as one of them, I'd love a summary." He smiled broadly.

I hadn't thought it possible to be less comfortable than I'd been a moment ago, but I was. I cleared my throat and thought about where to start.

"Come up here," Hugo said. He motioned to the floor next to the desk.

I didn't want to stand at the front of the class and talk about my business, not now, not ever. But I was the only person in the class properly informed about my situation, and if I left it to anyone else to recap the last class's discussion, the facts would get twisted. This was a point of pride, a chance to correct the record.

I walked to the front of the room and looked out at the students. Tex leaned back in his chair and watched me. I hadn't told him Mad for Mod had been under fire in my course, and now he was going to hear it here.

"Start with a quick summary about your business and your circumstances," Hugo said. "I'll interject with questions."

I nodded at him. "I'm Madison, and I run Mad for Mod, a boutique decorating business specializing in mid-century modern design. I'm a sole proprietor, and I recently lost my inventory in a legal battle. I have an empty showroom on Greenville Avenue and a decorating license and not much more."

"How long have you been in business?" the dean asked.

"Ten years," I said.

"How long have you turned a profit?"

"Ten years."

"Where did you get the start-up capital when you first launched?"

I'd described my business strategy enough times recently to summarize it quickly for the class finishing up with the dumpster-diving aspect of my business. "At first, I found items along the side of the road and either refinished them myself or hired a handyman to do the work."

"Low overhead. Good," the dean said.

"But not sustainable," Eric said. "She can't predict what people are going to throw out."

"Madison?" Hugo asked. "Care to respond?"

"He's right. I needed more inventory fast. I started reading the obituaries to identify women of a certain age, and I made offers to the next of kin to buy out the estate."

I've found my method for acquiring mid-century inventory elicited one of two responses in people: impressed by my outside-the-box thinking, or the more popular response: distaste for my opportunistic methods. In this case, two-thirds of the course went with the first, which made sense, this being Radical Business Strategy and all. It appeared I'd found my people.

Among the third of the class that didn't approve was Faye. I could see the disgust on her face. Her eyes were glossy, and she wiped at one—a tear?—and then balled up her fists and tucked them under her arms as if she were cold.

Nothing got past Hugo. "Faye, what do you think about Madison's methods?"

"It's disrespectful," she said. "Profiting from a family's loss."

"But I paid them. *They* profited. And by making an offer and arranging to take it all, I solved one of the biggest problems that falls onto the shoulders of adult children: what to do with Mom and Dad's stuff."

"People should honor the deceased, not talk about them in transactions." Blotches of red appeared on Faye's face, neck, and collarbone. She felt strongly about her opinion, and in the past, strong reactions to my methods usually indicated a person who had recently lost a loved one.

"If you can remove your emotions and think about it as a business transaction, you might see it differently," I said.

Faye stood up quickly and grabbed her things. "This makes me sick," she said and then ran out.

I STARED AT THE DOOR AFTER FAYE LEFT. I ALREADY KNEW people tended to disapprove of my methods, but to have a business student leave class after hearing them made me think twice. Was it possible potential clients were avoiding me because they didn't like the way I conducted business? Was my renegade thinking that off-putting?

The vacuum of silence that Faye's exit created was ended by Hugo. "Well," he said. "Radical business does create strong reactions." A few students laughed.

I stood awkwardly at the front of the class, unsure whether I were to remain where I was or if my time in the spotlight was over. The dean answered that question too. "Now that we know Madison's past, let's talk about her future. Where does she go from here?"

"Take time off and go to business school," called out a Mexican student in the back row, breaking the tension. The class laughed, Hugo among them. "Thank you, Octavio. I think Madison figured that step out already. Anybody else?"

"Declare bankruptcy, get out of her debts, and start a new company," a woman by the windows said.

"Go work for a big design firm," Eric contributed. It was the same suggestion he'd made in the previous discussion, and he was sticking to his guns.

Other suggestions followed, versions of what had already been said: start over, sell off, give up. The class had heard Gallagher's response, but none repeated it.

"And you, Madison? I imagine of everybody in this class, you've spent the most time thinking about this question. Do you agree with your classmates? Or do you have other ideas?"

I hadn't told anybody about my new ideas, but if not now, then when? I was surrounded by students interested in business planning. It was like facing a council of elders, except younger than me.

"I'm going to expand. Open a second studio. Take out a loan against my house and invest in inventory." I looked out at the expression of my peers, searching for support or approval.

"It'll never work," Tex said.

Tex. Said.

His was the one voice I hadn't expected to hear during class, and hearing it now, the lone critic of my plans, was like a punch to the gut. "Why not?" I asked. "I built the company once. I can do it again, and if I double down now, it'll take half as long to get back to where I was."

"That's just it," he said. "You built the company. Yourself. It was manageable for one woman then, but you're ten years older than you were, and you can't be in two places at once. If you open a second studio, you're going to have to hire a staff, and that's going to eat into your profits. You'll have to train them to do business the way you want and trust them to represent you to clients."

I felt hot and prickly, and it had nothing to do with menopause. "And what business are you in, *Rex?*"

He held my stare. It felt like there was nobody else in the room. He hadn't thought this part out, and I backed him into a corner.

"Madison, it isn't a requirement that students in this class are business owners," Hugo said at the same time Tex said, "Hats."

Both the dean and I turned to Tex. "Hats?" I repeated.

"Stetsons. Cowboy hats." He nodded at the dean.

Stetsons? I couldn't believe it. "Rex Stetson" was Rock Hudson's alter ego in *Pillow Talk!* The nerve of Tex using a Doris Day movie as part of his undercover operation.

"Well, that sounds interesting," Hugo said. His accent crept in a bit more than usual. He turned back to me. "You can sit down, Madison. I think we've spent enough time on you."

For the rest of the class, we touched upon risk assessment and projecting reward and had another heated discussion about forecasting, adjusted forecasts, and the reasons to change course mid-stream. I filled my notebook with pages of information and almost forgot about Tex in the back of the room. I guess there was a benefit to sitting in the front row after all.

As the clock neared eight thirty, the dean asked if there were any questions before we ended for the night. Eric held his hand up. "Professor Gallagher told us his book was assigned reading for this course. Do we still have to read it? And if not, will the bookstore give us credit for the return?"

"Which book was this?" Dean glanced down at the course lecture and spread the papers across the desk.

"*Rad Rage,*" Eric said.

"It's about how anger fuels radical thinking," said Octavio.

"He was right about it too. He used Madison as an example. She got mad when he told us about how her business failed, and she came up with bigger ideas than she started with. Right, Mad?"

He was right, and Gallagher had been right too. All of my ideas for expansion came after I got good and mad. My anger had been my fuel. "I haven't read his book yet, but you're right about my response."

Hugo's lips tightened. When he spoke, it was in a strained voice. "Professor Gallagher didn't clear his required reading through my office, so I'm going to have to get back to you," the dean said. He wrote something down. "On that note, let's call it a night." He turned to me and, in a lower voice, said, "Madison, can you stay behind for a few minutes?"

I nodded. Tex's explanation would have to wait.

The other classmates packed up their things and left. I was slow putting my books into my backpack. When I stood up and turned around, I saw Eric and Tex walking out together engrossed in conversation. Perhaps Tex dodged a bullet too.

"Madison, I know I put you on the spot today, and I wanted to thank you for your grace under pressure. I don't know why Professor Gallagher singled you out as a case study, but it makes for a good lesson plan for the class. Now, don't go listening to the fellow in the back row. He was just trying to get your goat. I don't know much about his hat company, but around here hats are easier to sell than water to a guy in a desert. Know what I mean?"

"I think so."

"This might sound unorthodox, but I like your moxie, and I think you're probably a good bet. I have some ideas for you that might not fall under the class curriculum. How about we get together to discuss them?"

Either the dean had taken an interest in my unique business proposition or he was using the moment for a unique proposition of an entirely different business—me. Several responses sprung to mind, from "I'm in a relationship" to "is it appropriate for the dean of the college to date a student?" But angered at Tex as I was, I knew it was smart to keep him out of this.

"That sounds nice. What time should I come to your office tomorrow?"

He laughed. "We don't need to spend office hours on this. There's a club not far from campus. We could go there now."

"Now?" I said a bit too harshly. "I can't go anywhere now," I added in a softer voice. I patted my backpack. "I've got an awful lot of homework," I said. "Between my entry level courses and now this one at night, I don't want to slip behind."

"I see." His face fell. "Yes, I suppose you have a lot on your plate. Okay. Well, then. Office hours it will be."

I hoisted my bag onto my shoulder and made it to the door before he called out behind me. "Oh, Madison? I understand you're the student who found Professor Gallagher's body. As you can see, there's going to be gossip about what happened. I'd consider it a personal favor if you kept what you know to yourself."

Whether it was the guilt over my rejection or the power dynamic of him being my professor, I quickly acquiesced. "Of course," I said, though it wasn't until I was at my car that I wondered why he cared.

13

On the bright side, getting out of class at eight thirty at night allowed me to completely miss rush hour, though Rocky wouldn't be happy. Even with long walks both morning and night, he probably felt neglected.

I was surprised to find Tex's Jeep parked by my house. I was more surprised to find him sitting inside it waiting for my arrival. I parked my Alfa Romeo and approached him. My surprise was tempered with residual anger; I was still mad at his criticism of my plan.

He had his arm dangling out of the driver's-side window. "I told you not to go back to class, Night."

"You of all people know how important this is to me. Do you think it's easy to let a classroom full of strangers attack me?"

"This isn't about your MBA. It's a police investigation. You heard Ms. Talbot."

"Who?"

"The blonde. Her name is Faye Talbot. She was right. Mr.

Gallagher was murdered. Until we find out who murdered him, that campus isn't safe."

Tex had an unfair way of winning every argument by reminding me his actions were driven by loftier goals than mine, but I was too mad to give in so quickly.

"That explains why you would send an officer to question the students or even assign a detective to go undercover but not why it had to be you." I crossed my arms. "Is that why you wanted me to drop the class? Don't worry, Captain. I won't blow your cover."

"Are you going back to class tomorrow night?"

"Of course, I'm going back to class tomorrow night. I was there first!" I turned around and left him there.

"Night," he called. "We're not done talking about this."

"You can wait. I have to check on Rocky."

But before I had the house unlocked, Tex's Jeep peeled out down the road.

Complications upon complications upon complications. That was how life felt. I had a business, then I lost my business, and now I wanted my business back.

I didn't have a relationship with Tex, then I did have a relationship with Tex, but now it seemed we were at odds once again.

I had a sweet, peppy, affectionate Shih Tzu puppy, and at least that hadn't changed. Rocky was as steadfast as, well, a rock. We went out for a walk (and two separate deposits in the garden) and had a snack (peanut butter for him and a couple of cookies from a fresh box of Peanut Butter Patties for me.). Rocky required less fuss to get ready for bed, so I left him with his rope bone and showered off the day then dressed in a set of mint green silk pajamas previously owned by Thelma Johnson herself. Of all the deceased women whose clothes I wore, I knew the most about her.

I came to her through the obituaries. I entertained a brief memory of her son hanging up on me when I first made an offer on the estate. He'd thought it was a joke. A few minutes later he called back, accepted, and thanked me. We both won. I won further when he gave me this house. You could argue I wouldn't be where I was today if not for the obituaries. If not for my interaction with Thelma Johnson's son, I might still be living in my apartment building. Was I willing to risk everything I had to expand the business everyone else seemed to think was a sinking ship?

I went downstairs and unpacked my backpack, but I wasn't of the mindset to tackle homework. I pulled Professor Gallagher's book out and carried it upstairs. I climbed into the bed and Rocky jumped on top, and while the book seemed interesting, I'm embarrassed to say I didn't make it through the introduction before falling asleep.

THE RINGING PHONE didn't wake me in the middle of the night. It didn't wake me in the morning either. That was not a statement of how soundly I slept but about the absence of calls. I took Rocky with me to the swim club and dropped him off in the dog room, swam for an hour, and then collected him and drove home. There would be no Round Two with Tex.

I dressed in a sleeveless pink A-line dress with a bow at the collar, white daisy earrings with pink centers, and white Keds. Having my Radical Business Strategy course moved to night left me with a leisurely morning, so I poured a fresh cup of coffee and reviewed my class notes for Decision-Making for the Business Leader. The material was dry, and I welcomed the sound of the doorbell. It was Dennis, the realtor.

"Good morning," he said. "I wasn't sure whether we were going to meet here or next door."

I'd been so focused on what I could do with the property that I'd forgotten all about my scheduled walk-through. "I guess it's good that I live next door." I smiled.

He declined my offer of coffee, so I left my mug on the table. I clipped on Rocky's leash and led him through the living and sitting rooms (old houses were funny that way) and out the front door. It was an entrance I rarely used but that put us on the sidewalk in front of the vacant property.

Rocky trotted in front of us and sniffed the sidewalk. A cardinal sat on the For Sale sign. A sign on a sign? I shook off the thought. If this was a business decision, then it had to be made with cold, hard facts, not because of a pretty red bird.

Dennis fumbled with the key to the lockbox, and for a moment I worried once again he'd brought the wrong key. Eventually the lockbox opened. He unlocked the building and entered. Rocky and I followed.

The interior smelled musty. Dennis pushed the curtains on the windows aside and then hand-cranked the window to open it. Natural light filled the interior. It was a cavernous square filled with boxes.

"Thelma Johnson sold it after her husband died. The new owners never had a chance to use it. When Hurricane Alicia hit in '83, the damage was extensive. The insurance money covered their losses, but they reopened elsewhere and let the place sit. It's been paid off for decades and occasionally pops up on the market, but it's a weird little commercially zoned building on a small property in a residential neighborhood, and these days, that's three strikes."

Aside from the curtains, which were lined in coated cotton, there were few fabrics in the interior, which made our voices carry. Cardboard boxes were stacked haphazardly along the back wall. Several had visible damage. I walked away from Dennis to the window facing my house. When I looked out, I could see the yellow and white daisy curtains hanging in my kitchen. A bright yellow butterfly passed the window in an erratic flight pattern, and I watched it until it disappeared from view. I left the window and walked to the back of the building.

A small kitchenette, complete with two burners, and a powder room were at the back by a rear door. I turned the knob and pulled the door open. The gray cat sat outside looking in. It startled me so much I shut the door quickly. When I opened it again, the cat trotted away.

I closed and locked the door and returned to the musty interior. "How much are they asking?"

"Before we talk price, we should talk damage," he said. "The foundation has sunk, so it's going to need to be supported. Two jacks, maybe more. The price is as-is, so repairs would fall on you."

"It's a fixer-upper," I said.

The longer I wandered the interior, the more I knew this was a decision I didn't need to sleep on. Three days of business school pointed at one thing: I already knew how to run a business, and I knew it by doing it. The most passionate I'd felt in the past month was in class and with Tex—it was his unexpected lack of belief in me that set me off last night—but that told me I still had the fire to make this work. And if the real estate mantra of "location, location, location" was true, then this was a bullseye. It was thirty feet from my house.

"Let's do it," I said. "Draw up the paperwork and see how much equity I have in Thelma Johnson's house. But do me one favor: keep this quiet. I don't want anyone to know the new owner is me."

"Won't it be obvious when you move your showroom here?"

"I'm not going to move my showroom. Find out what I need to make an offer, and I'll go from there."

14

———

Dennis and I went in different directions. I repacked the books I'd left out on my kitchen table into my backpack and added a ham and cheese sandwich on rye. Those vending machines were going to leave me broke, and if things went according to plan, I was looking at a new level of financial risk. Professor Gallagher would be proud.

Creature of habit that I sometimes was, I parked in Lot B and walked to the Canfield building.

Barbara greeted me at the admissions desk. "Madison, I have a message for you." She turned her back and leaned over the desk to retrieve a folded piece of paper. She straightened and extended it to me. "Dean Wallace asked me to give that to you." Her expression was disapproving, which hinted that she'd already peeked inside.

"Thank you." I took the paper but didn't open it in her presence. There seemed no point in letting her see my reaction. "Have there been any new updates to the curriculum?"

"If there had been, there would be a notification on your student profile. Have you logged into the portal today?"

"Not yet."

"Don't be like the kids, Madison. Make it a habit. You won't always get preferential treatment."

"Am I getting preferential treatment now?" I asked. Her eyes shifted to the paper in my hand and back to my face. It was so quick I didn't think she realized she'd done it, but I was more curious than before to walk away and see what the note said.

The door behind her opened, and Hugo strode in. Today he wore a tan suit and cowboy boots. His white shirt was unbuttoned at the neck, revealing a white undershirt. "Madison. Good to see you back at school. Did you get my message?"

I held up the piece of paper. "This?"

"Good." He stood behind Barbara, and she seemed to have created a task to keep her from looking at him or me. "I was hoping to talk to you after class," he said. He glanced at his watch, a brushed gold face on a well-worn brown leather strap. "But I can spare a few minutes now." He walked through the maze of desks in the office and paused by the stout office manager. "Barbara, you're looking very smart today."

She turned around. "Don't waste your sweet talk," she said. "I've worked here too long for charm to work on me."

Hugo smiled as though he got the response he'd wanted. He flipped the counter up and walked through and then eased it back into place.

We walked side by side down the hallway to his office. "I've been thinking about your predicament since last night," he said.

"Which predicament is that?" I asked innocently. It had been a busy twelve hours for predicaments!

He turned the knob to his office door and pushed it inside

then stood back and let me enter first. He closed the door behind him. "Have a seat. I won't keep you long, but there's no reason to stand on ceremony."

I sat in front of his desk, and he sat behind it. The chairs were calibrated to varying heights, putting him in a position of dominance. I'm not sure why I was surprised; he *was* the dean of the business school, after all.

"I took the liberty of checking your schedule," he said. "You've packed it pretty tight."

"My bachelor's degree was in General Studies," I said.

"From here?" he asked, pointing to the college grounds.

"No, from a university in Pennsylvania. Two, actually." I spared him the details of dropping and eventually filling in the course requirements needed to quietly graduate. "I relocated to Texas after that."

"Why do you want an MBA?"

"You heard about my business in class last night. I need a loan to get me back on my feet, but the banks don't see me as a good risk. I've turned a profit since the day I opened, but every move I've made was based on instinct, not practical business strategy. An MBA would show them they were wrong."

"Business is like sex. If done correctly, nothing about it should be practical."

I wondered briefly if I'd treated my loan applications with this in mind, would the decisions have turned out differently? Perish the thought!

"Will that be covered in class?" I asked with feigned innocence.

"I'm still working out the new syllabus," Hugo said absent-mindedly. He leaned back in his chair. It tipped at an extreme angle and creaked. He laced his fingers together and rested them across the mother-of-pearl buttons on his shirt. It was the same body language Professor Gallagher had adopted the day we met. "Depending on your transcript, you might be missing some qualifications, but if you have run a successful business, I can give you credit for the experience. That'll free up your days for more pressing matters."

"That would be fantastic," I said without filter.

"Go to class as usual and I'll talk to your professors. I may have an answer for you after class tonight."

"Thank you, Dean Wallace."

He chuckled. "You're welcome, Student Madison." He slapped his fingertips against the desk. "Time's up You're already late for your eleven o'clock."

I sat through Decision-Making for the Business Leader and thought about how drastically things had changed for me in a matter of days. Earlier this week, I talked my way into Professor Gallagher's course, and already I was poised to act on what we'd discussed. Hugo Wallace was nicer than Professor Gallagher, but he lacked the killer instinct I'd felt from the passionate professor in my one and only class with him. My mind wandered back to Monday, when we'd been alone in the parking structure.

I'd spent much of my time since then thinking about my business, and all of those thoughts had been triggered by Gallagher's lecture. My embarrassment had quickly turned to the fire that fueled my plans, and in a matter of days I was looking at a completely different reality. But what if I hadn't been so quick to get on board? Would his use of my company as an example for the class made me resentful enough to kill him?

It seemed unlikely. But the way Gallagher had died left me with questions. He'd said the break-in to his car was the third time this month. Someone had wanted to make life difficult for him. Was the break-in connected to the clogged tailpipe? Had murder been the endgame for the vandal, or had the entire set-up been meant as a threat? Nasty had said the car would have stalled or blown out whatever was clogging the tailpipe, so why had it continued to run?

The memory felt like a series of pictures taken of the same subject at different times, torn apart and then pieced back together from mismatched originals. If Tex had results from the forensic automotive specialist, he wouldn't mention them to me. I should forget about it and focus on my classes, but the two had become intertwined. I couldn't shake the belief that Gallagher's death was linked to the school.

Secure in the anonymity of the lecture hall, I tuned out the professor and flipped to a fresh page in my notebook. I'd had few interactions with Gallagher, but details about him had come to me through a variety of sources. He shared an office with Ansel Benedict. Barbara implied he had improper relations with female students, and Hugo claimed his syllabus was controversial. Tex said a deep dive into Gallagher's background had revealed similar things: sexual harassment complaints leading to termination from a different college. If he hadn't literally written the book on radical thinking, I would have dismissed his credentials. But despite all of this, I recognized that it was Gallagher's aggressive teaching style that had shaken me out of my malaise. I felt the loss of him even though I'd barely known him.

As my mind wandered, a student in the third row raised

her hand. When called on, she asked her question, but from my seat in the back of the class, I couldn't hear. The guy two seats next to me cupped his hands around his mouth and called out, "Louder." A few other students mimicked the request.

The professor gestured for the student to stand. It wasn't until then I recognized Faye.

"I asked under what circumstances should a business owner make a decision that's unpopular with her team? If she feels strongly, is it worth alienating the people around her to follow her instincts, or should she try to convince them she's right?"

"That's a good discussion point," the professor said, "and I'd like everybody in this class to be prepared to answer it in essay form. One thousand words. Due Monday."

Eric, who had been assisting the professor during class, leaned forward and said something to the professor. He nodded and addressed the class again. "You get a one-day reprieve. Monday classes were canceled out of respect for Professor Gallagher. Essays due Tuesday. And since you have an extra day, let's make it eight hundred words. This isn't English Lit. There's a benefit to making your argument in fewer words, not more."

A collective groan went up around the class. "Thank you, Ms. Talbot. Class dismissed."

I remained in my seat and kept my eyes on Faye. Judging from the number of people who ignored her while streaming out of the class, she was persona non grata amongst her fellow students. I let the room clear out and then waited for her to pass me.

"Faye," I called out. She turned to me, and I added, "I'm Madison. We're in Radical Business Strategy together."

"Oh. Yes. Sure." She looked like she hadn't gotten much sleep. "Are you going to say something too?"

"About your question? No, I think it was valid. People who work for themselves don't think about things like that, but if they plan to expand somewhere in the future, it's probably better to know how to handle the situation earlier rather than when it comes up."

"Right," she said, considering me in a new light. "You're totally right. That's what I wanted to know." She rolled her eyes. "And now it looks like another all-nighter."

"It won't take you all night to write that essay," I said. "We can write them together if you want. After class tonight. We can critique each other's and make them better before we turn them in."

She frowned. "I won't be in class tonight," she said. "I'm dropping out. Dean Wallace said I wasn't a fit for the subject matter. It was either drop the class or fail it, and if I fail, I'll lose my scholarship."

"Dean Wallace said that?"

"He said he reviewed Professor Gallagher's notes on the class, and it was in my file. I wish the professor had told me himself."

"Would it have been different hearing it from him?"

"It might have made a big difference to both of us."

15

FAYE LED THE WAY OUT OF THE LECTURE HALL. "THANKS FOR the offer, though. Good luck." She ended on a surprising up note and disappeared into a swarm of students.

My offer to meet with Faye hadn't been completely for her benefit. I'd been hoping to talk about Professor Gallagher. Aside from the rumor of suicide, there'd been remarkably little said about him. It was as if the college mandated a confidentiality clause on the subject. It was probably somewhere on the student portal.

The rest of my day passed in a blur of classes, coffee, and my ham sandwich. I bought a bag of chips to go with it, thus breaking my vending machine boycott. There were times when my willpower was undeniably weak.

When Statistics ended, I stayed in my seat and worked on my essay. I didn't know whether I would see Tex tonight or not, but being first in class felt like staking my claim on it. I felt adversarial, so I sat at the desk he'd occupied the day before, knowing it would force him to sit up front. The move

111

was inspired in part by our class; required reading had included Sun Tzu's *The Art of War.*

As students filtered into the class, I watched the door. Tex and Eric rounded the corner together. Eric handed Tex a flyer. The images were familiar. It was what Eric had been copying that he hadn't wanted me to see. I smiled to myself, remembering I had the master in my backpack.

Tex was so engrossed in his conversation with Eric that he didn't see me until he was a foot away from me. "You're at my desk," he said.

"Last time I looked, there weren't assigned seats."

He adjusted his stack of books and leaned down. "You're not making this easy," he said.

Before I could respond, Hugo entered the class. "Take your seats, everyone." He walked to the front of the class and looked at my empty desk then looked out at the room. When he saw me talking to Tex, he frowned. "Rex, come on up to the front of the class. Let's give Madison the night off and dissect your business tonight."

"I don't think that's a good idea," Tex said.

"Sure, it is," Hugo said. "We rarely get the chance to use real live businesses for discussion, and in this class we have two."

"Three," Eric said. We turned to him. "I manage an events company."

"Yes. Be that as it may, let's use Rex Allen's company as our example. Rex, come on up here and give the class a thumbnail sketch of your business."

Tex walked to the front of the room and set his books on what had been my desk. He stood next to the dean and put his hands in his pockets. As angry as I was with him, I recognized how close he was to blowing his cover. I raised my hand. "Dean?" I called out.

"Yes, Madison?"

"I got a surprising amount of forward momentum based on the class discussions and would love if the class kept brainstorming about Mad for Mod."

"I'm sure you would," Eric muttered loud enough for the class to hear.

"We can talk about your business after class tonight."

If I gained sympathy by volunteering to take the bullet with Tex's name on it, I'd never know. The mention of the dean meeting with me after class caused a dark cloud to pass over Tex's features, and then his unreadable cop face slipped into place. It was like watching a person morph into a clone of themselves: there in physical presence but not in emotion.

He stood with his feet shoulder width apart. His hands stayed in his pockets, just the fingers, and his wrists relaxed. For anyone who didn't know him, he seemed like an everyday guy who suddenly was thrust into the spotlight. His acting wasn't bad.

I was so focused on Tex's performance I didn't realize someone had entered the room until I saw Tex stare at the doorway. I followed his stare and saw one of the homicide detectives, Ling, standing inside the door. She rapped her knuckles against the doorframe.

"I'm sorry to interrupt your class," she said. She moved her blazer to the side to show the badge clipped to the waistband of her black trousers. "Ling Tsu with the Lakewood Police Department. I need to talk to Madison Night, and I heard she was here." Ling shifted her attention from Tex and Hugo at the front of the room to the rows of seated students. "Ms. Night?" she asked.

Whether it was because I was in the back row or because Tex instructed her to pretend she didn't already know me, she waited for me to identify myself. I raised my arm. "I'm Madison Night," I said.

"Can you get your things and come with me?"

The request was routine. She was investigating Professor Gallagher's murder, and I was the one who'd found the body. But she could have found me at any time during the day. Tex knew my schedule. This well-timed visit and request for me to leave accomplished one thing Tex wanted: it got me out of the classroom.

I couldn't help myself; I looked directly at him. Fortunately for both of us, Hugo was at the front of the room with him and mistook my reaction as seeking his approval.

"Go ahead, Madison," the dean said. "I'll catch you up on the lesson plan when you're done."

Tex stared at me. Most of the class stared at me, so Tex's attention wasn't suspicious. But it felt like a chess move and I was the rook. He'd maneuvered things so I was no longer in the game.

Arguing would have raised questions I wasn't prepared to answer, so I nodded and stood, packed my books into my bag and left. I joined Ling by the door, and she stood back and let me exit first. She turned back to the front of the room. "Thank you for cooperating," she said. She closed the classroom door behind her.

"Where can we talk?" she asked.

"In here," I said, pointing at an empty classroom. It was the room where Ansel Benedict taught his drama course. He'd mentioned the grudge match between himself and Gallagher, but his involvement with the local theater would have kept him from teaching a course at night. I turned the knob and went inside.

Unlike the classroom where Radical Business Strategy took place, Ansel's room was a study in theater. Two floor-to-ceiling bookcases lined the back wall and were filled with bound scripts from classic productions. A row of mannequins in costume were positioned by the window, and the teacher's desk was clean save for brass masks to represent comedy and tragedy. The chairs, instead of being set up in typical classroom formation toward the front, had been rearranged in a circle. One chair had a pink windbreaker draped on the back of it. College students were always leaving things behind.

"Can they hear us?" Ling asked, pointing at the wall.

"The professor who uses this room had it soundproofed."

"I've never heard of a classroom being soundproofed."

"You've never met Ansel Benedict."

She pulled out her phone and raised it to her face. "Talk to Ansel Benedict," she said.

"Voice memo?"

"No. Sue's listening in." She held her phone up, and I saw "Sue Two" on the screen.

"Is that ethical?"

"Calling a friend? Sure, why not?" The sound of laughter trickled from the phone. "Captain Allen said you might put up an argument when I pulled you out of class. Sue wanted to listen in." She held the phone close to her mouth and said, "I'll fill you in tomorrow," then she hung up.

"You don't have questions for me about Professor Gallagher's murder, do you?" I asked. "That was just a way to get me out of the room."

"There are a few things you should know about Mr.

Gallagher's murder, and Captain Allen thought this was the best way to clue you in."

It wasn't in Tex's usual bag of tricks to keep me abreast of the findings in a murder investigation, and if he did want me to know what was going on, he could have told me. There was something else behind Ling's visit.

"Tell me what you saw when Mr. Gallagher died."

I recounted the memory. "There was something jammed into the tailpipe of his car. His passenger-side door wouldn't stay closed because someone had broken into it, so I gave him my scarf to tie it down from the inside. About a minute after he did that, he slumped over his seatbelt and died."

"Here's what we know from the toxicology report and early findings. Mr. Gallagher had taken a large dose of sedatives. Lloyd's trying to establish a timeline, but the adrenaline he would have felt after finding his car vandalized would have increased blood flow and caused them to absorb faster."

"Then you can rule out suicide."

She held up her hand. "You saw something in his tailpipe. Normally, the car would have blown it out or stalled. The forensic automotive specialist discovered a hole drilled into his exhaust pipe and a hose that directed the exhaust back into the cabin of the vehicle via a second hole drilled into the floorboards."

I was more surprised by how on-the-nose Nasty had been with her working theory than I was with the facts themselves. I looked away from Ling and put the pieces together. "Someone rerouted the deadly emissions to the cabin of the car so he would die from asphyxiation. They drugged him ahead of time so he'd already be sleepy. But what about the vandalism? How does that play into everything? Surely if the car door wouldn't stay closed, noxious gas fumes couldn't build up and kill him."

"That's where we're having trouble too. If someone wanted him dead, they couldn't predict you'd come along and offer him your scarf when you did. There might be a witness who saw what was about to go down and broke into the car to counter the effects of the gas, or a student who saw an opportunity to steal files from the professor's car. The killer might have had second thoughts or a crisis of conscience. Right now, we're swimming in theories."

"Couldn't a witness—or a killer with second thoughts—just take the rag out of the tailpipe?"

"That would make more sense than our theories, yes."

I sat silent for a moment, trying to understand the killer's motivation. Had what happened to Gallagher been meant as a warning? Was this a scare tactic gone wrong? A murder plot with a regretful murderer? A lovers' quarrel gone too far?

"What now?" I asked. "The case seems far from solved."

"Now we shake trees and interview suspects. Captain Allen continues to work this thing from the inside."

"What about me?"

"Captain Allen can't tell you what to do, but he did want you to know from what we've figured out, every person in your class is under suspicion."

16

I narrowed my eyes. "Are you here on official police business?" I asked Ling.

"Let's call it a favor for a friend." She smiled. "Nobody wants to see you get hurt, Madison, least of all Captain Allen. He could have sent any number of detectives to the school to go undercover, but he wanted to do it himself. He has a reputation as a hard-headed dinosaur, but there's a reason both Sue and I wanted to work for him." She studied me for a moment and then added, "And there's a reason you wanted to date him."

There was one thing you didn't get with male cops: relationship insights.

After the city's first round of budget cuts castrated the Lakewood Police Department, Tex's officers were spread too thin to get a handle on the rising crime rate. Petty crime rates rose because there weren't enough cops to catch the perpetrators.

Traffic violations, once considered a nuisance, became the

most reliable way for police departments to meet their income quotas. Tex didn't go that route. He networked with wealthy residents and lobbied for donations. He didn't just solicit the old-school Dallas wealthy either. He sent his officers out into the communities that had been growing among pockets of the Lakewood/White Rock Lake community, had them get to know the residents and found out what they wanted from their police. It was a bold public relation move that paid off. His precinct gained a reputation for acceptance and tolerance, and minority-owned businesses showed their support.

In a chicken-or-egg scenario, the donations gave him the power to recruit, and the officers who answered the call were of a new generation. In the span of five years, the Lakewood Police Department had gone from the boys' club that drove out Nasty when she was the sole female officer to one of the most diverse in the county. Ling Tsu and Sue Niedermeyer were part of that wave, and their success was better than any recruiting tactics Tex could dream up.

"He could have told me he was going to be here," I said.

"No, he couldn't. Telling you would have compromised the investigation."

"But you're telling me now," I said.

"I'm the officer who took your initial statement. This is a follow-up conversation."

It made sense, but it didn't make me happy. "The dean is looking into giving me course credit for my business experience," I said. "If that happens, I'll have one class left." I pointed at the room next to us. "And if I drop that class, I'll be dropping out of school completely."

Ling leaned forward and propped her chin on her fist. "If the school gives you course credit for your experience, doesn't that indicate you already know what they're teaching?"

I didn't know how to explain the rejections from the banks or the feeling that one dumb mistake had cost me everything. I'd charged headfirst into my business, and I made it work, but because of the lawsuit, I lost my confidence. Maybe that was it.

"Do you know I was sued?" I remembered the saying I'd heard around the precinct when the two Sues got a confession from a criminal: *you've been Sued.* "I mean, the lawsuit. You've heard about it, right?"

"We all heard about it. Madison, you lost your idol, and you weren't thinking straight. You made a mistake, and it changed things." She sat up straight. "My grandfather used to teach me Chinese proverbs when I was growing up. He said, 'He who returns from a journey is not the same as he who left.' You're not the same person who started your company ten years ago. You probably learned more in those ten years than you ever will at this school."

I thanked Ling, and we left the classroom together. I was surprised to discover how loud Radical Business Strategy was once we opened the door. Ansel was right to soundproof his room; the noise level would have been disruptive to a class of would-be thespians trying to get into character.

Ling offered to walk me out to my car. I recognized the gesture as a thinly veiled way to ensure I left the campus, and I called her out on it. "I need to talk to the dean," I said. "If I'm going to drop out, he shouldn't waste his time fighting to get me course credit for my experience."

"Good point. Take care, Madison."

I sat on a bench outside class and listened to the discussion. If I just wanted to learn with no obligation to pay tuition or obtain a degree, I could audit the course from the hallway. The voices carried easily. They were discussing bold business moves that had paid off big for investors.

Again, I felt a tingle of excitement. I opened my notebook, now filled more with notes for Mad for Mod than any lectures I'd attended, and I created a sample budget. What would it look like if I bought the property next to Thelma Johnson's house? How deep in debt would I be if I kept the storefront on Greenville Avenue too? Could I afford to transition my lone part-time employee to a salaried position and train her to run the place in my absence? Did I want that?

It had been a long time since my creative juices were flowing, and with no place else to go, they went into my plans. It was a brain dump, pure and simple. Unconnected thoughts flowed out of me and onto the page. *Pro bono work in exchange for client testimonials. Adjunct location: specialize in bathrooms and kitchens? Danish Modern? Atomic? Rent out space for local artisans? Learn skills for business: reupholstery? Solicit referrals from existing clients.*

But the thing that fired me up more than making lists and plans about how to expand was doing the work again. I thought about how I felt at the bank, sitting in front of the loan officer, and knowing how easy it would have been to craft a renovation proposal for them.

I closed my eyes and rested my pen on my notebook. I could see it: buff the existing travertine walls and polish the poured terrazzo floors. Bring in Saarinen tables for brochures and check signing stations. It would be spectacular. A destination spot. People would go to the Dallas First National Bank just to see the interior.

Except they wouldn't. Who went to a bank to look at the furniture?

I tore the page out of my notebook and crumbled it up. I didn't need the bank to give me a job. I needed them to give me a loan.

I pulled out my phone and saw a missed call from Dennis. His message said to call him back.

As the class debated the pros and cons of bankruptcy behind me, I stood from the bench and wandered into the hallway and returned the realtor's call.

"Dennis? This is Madison Night."

"Yes. One minute." The phone went silent. Several seconds later, Dennis returned. "Sorry about that. Family movie night."

"I'm sorry to disturb you at home."

"It's fine," he said. "The kids picked *The Incredibles* for the twenty-third time," he said. I laughed. "I'm not joking. My oldest keeps a logbook."

"Future statistician?"

"Future something." Dennis paused a moment and then continued. "Madison, I hate to do this over the phone, but with your hectic schedule, I wasn't sure when we'd connect. I heard back from the bank."

"Already? Don't I need to fill out paperwork before they approve my loan?"

"I have your information on file. I made a couple of calls first, just to feel out your situation before we made an official offer on the place and, well, there's a problem."

"What problem?" I asked. The excited tingle in my chest from earlier turned to tightness. I tapped my sternum and stopped pacing. "Surely there's enough equity in Thelma Johnson's house to start the process."

"That was what I thought too, but I didn't realize you bought and renovated the apartment building on Gaston Avenue. Your debt-to-income ratio is out of whack, and the banks aren't comfortable with the odds of you meeting your payment schedule."

"That's not fair!" I cried out. My voice bounced off the walls of the hallway and magnified. "Did you tell them I'm getting my MBA? That I'm committed to expansion of my existing decorating business? They should see if I'm willing to borrow against the equity of my house I'm serious. I'm not going to do anything to jeopardize where I live."

"I'm sorry, Madison, but it's not simply good business, it's ethics. You have too much to lose."

I dropped onto the bench next to the vending machine. This wasn't how this conversation was supposed to go. Dennis's enthusiasm had opened a door for optimism, and now, the newest rejection was more crushing than the rest of them combined.

"What do I do now?" I asked.

"The sooner you show the bank you can bring in money, the sooner they'll change their mind. Get back out there, Madison. You still have the showroom on Greenville. Start there."

We ended the call on a cordial note. Dennis hadn't known I bought back the building he helped me sell, and that might have made him rethink me as a loyal client. But a realtor's opinion of me wasn't among the ten biggest problems I had.

I kicked my feet out in front of me and slouched down on the bench. What was I doing in night school? Nobody thought this was a good idea. Maybe they were right. The time I spent here wasn't helping me get back on my feet—it was a distraction. I should forget trying to learn something new about business and double down on what I knew. Dumpster diving it was.

In the background, I heard a door open and the sound of

people filling the hallway. Class had run a few minutes longer than usual, but now it was over. I put away my phone and notebook and waited until the sounds subsided before slowly making my way back to the room. The room had emptied except for the dean and two male students who appeared to be wrapping up their conversation.

As I walked in, I saw Tex's Jeep keys on the floor under his (formerly my) desk. He couldn't leave without them. Without thinking, I scooped them up, then I remembered I had no reason to know "Rex," no ability to contact him about his lost keys. I set them on the desk surface.

The dean and the students finished up, and the students left.

"Madison," Hugo said. "I'm glad you came back. I wanted to talk to you about something."

"I need to talk to you about something too." I steeled myself. "I'm having doubts about whether business school is the right decision for me. When we spoke earlier, you said you were going to look into giving me course credit for my experience, but I don't want you to waste your time."

"Are you saying you're withdrawing from Van Doren College?"

Was that what I was saying? "I don't know. I need to think about it before I can give you an answer."

"Fair enough." He closed his textbook and stood straight. "I can't say I want you to leave, but your decision does make what I wanted to say easier."

Great. More bad news? What now?

"Yes?"

"Have dinner with me tomorrow night. I have a—a decorating dilemma. You may be the perfect person to help me out."

"You want to hire me?"

"I need someone like you, Madison. Meet me outside Canfield. I'd love to tell you more." Hugo looked over my shoulder. "Rex? Did you forget something?"

I turned around and saw Tex in the doorway. He pointed at the keys on the desk next to me. "Keys," he said. "Must have fallen out of my pocket."

"Can't get far without them," the dean said.

"No siree." Tex scooped them up and pocketed them. His eyes moved back and forth between the dean and me. "Ma'am?" He hesitated. "I'll walk you to your car if you like."

"Thank you," I said. I turned to the dean. "And thank you for understanding."

I walked toward Tex, gauging his body language for hostility. Behind me, Hugo said, "See you in class Rex. And you, Madison? Will I see you tomorrow night?"

Heat flushed my face. "Tomorrow night. Yes."

"Great. It's a date."

Cue hostility in five-four-three-two-one.

17

I'VE NEVER BEEN SO AWARE OF MY FEET MOVING ONE STEP IN front of the other. Tex and I walked side by side, but to anyone watching, we were strangers who happened to attend the same class. His hostility didn't just work on a granular level; it suited his undercover story as well.

By the time we reached my car, I'd stopped focusing on my footsteps and started cycling through various conversation points. I even considered asking Tex to tell me about his hat business, since Ling had effectively removed me from the classroom right about when the dean aimed the spotlight in Tex's direction. But having a conversation about fictitious lives was like living in a house of cards. The illusion would last until it crashed down around us.

A pair of campus police officers stood in the parking structure about thirty feet from my car. I nodded at them. One was the officer who had responded to my call the day Professor Gallagher died. He nodded back. Tex ignored them both.

"I don't suppose I have to ask which car is yours," he said.

I mistakenly thought he had worked past his hostility. I smiled. "Are you hungry? Do you want to get something to eat?"

My voice carried through the empty parking structure, and the campus police officers turned toward us.

"Ma'am, I appreciate the offer," Tex said, "but this assignment is going to put a crimp in my social life."

"Oh. Yes. Of course," I stammered. And then I added, "You have my number in the event those notes I gave you weren't clear. I'm a morning person, so I prefer you don't call after nine."

"I'll keep that in mind."

"Thank you for the escort. Good night, Rex."

"Good night, Madison."

See, now, this was silly. Most of the time, Tex called me by my last name. I'd never corrected him or minded, frankly. It was part of the way we communicated from the start and he hadn't changed the habit when we shifted into friendlier relations.

I rarely heard him say my first name. Maybe that was why tonight, in the dark parking structure, with two campus police officers who probably shouldn't know Tex and I weren't strangers, the sound of him saying it gave me a thrill. It felt intimate, like we were role-playing. Which at least one of us was.

Tex appeared to have the same reaction. The moment he spoke my name, his pupils dilated. His eyes dropped from mine to my lips, where they remained. My heartbeat, which had been in treadmill-zone since I spoke to Dennis, thumped in my chest. The air around us felt charged, which made it more difficult to pretend we were strangers.

"I suppose I should go home now," I said.

"I suppose you should," he replied. He raised his hand halfway as if he were about to touch me but then stopped. "I almost forgot. You missed out on the assignment."

Tex pulled out a notebook from the bottom of his stack of books and put it on top. He tore out a sheet of paper out and scribbled something on it and then folded it and handed it to me. "If you haven't been keeping up with the reading, you'll want to get on that immediately. There might be a quiz."

"Thank you." I unlocked my car and climbed in.

Tex, selling the role of chivalrous gentleman, waited in the parking structure to make sure my car started. I drove away and left him alone with the campus police. I waited until I had left the college campus to read his note.

Until this case is solved, I can't risk blowing my cover. Don't put your life on hold.

That was the secret, romantic note Tex handed me?

A car horn honked behind me. I tossed the note on the passenger seat and pulled forward then drove home with my blood boiling. *Don't put your life on hold.* What was that—permission? Did he think I wasn't mature enough to wait out a homicide investigation? Or was this his way of saying his "cover" was an excuse to indulge in his old bachelor behavior?

I got home and let Rocky out. Since our parent/puppy hours had shifted to later nights, I'd swapped out his usual collar for a glow-in-the-dark one so I could keep track of him more easily. He ran down the stairs and into the yard, circled the Japanese maple tree a few times, and pooped on an exposed root. It was my yard, and I was tired, and what harm would come of leaving it there to fertilize the ground?

I sat on a partially rusted two-seater swing in my yard and watched Rocky's glow-in-the-dark collar dart around in the darkness. I used to feel like that. Like everything was shiny and new and there were opportunities all around me. I had steady work and more inventory than I could manage thanks to curbside finds, obituary purchases, and weekends of flea marketing. When I didn't have clients, I'd remerchandise my showroom window. I repainted rooms more often than some people spackled, and little by little, I built up a reputation so solid the local paint store asked me to endorse a collection of paint colors.

I sat up a little straighter. Why hadn't I thought about that? Mitchell Moore, the owner of Paintin' Place, wasn't just a business contact. He was a friend. My endorsement deal had been an experiment, and the last time we spoke, he was on his seventh reorder. I may not be getting my MBA anytime soon, but that didn't mean I couldn't recognize a smart business move when I saw it.

***

THE NEXT MORNING, with no classes to attend, I decided to indulge in some woman-dog bonding time. I dressed in a peach shirtwaist dress, another item from the kindergarten teacher's wardrobe, and clipped a matching leash onto Rocky's collar, and we left. He hung his head out the window while I drove to the Casa Linda Shopping Center where Paintin' Place resided.

I entered the paint store and found Mitchell behind the counter mixing paint. The machine made it impossible to converse, so I waved at him and browsed the paint swatches while he finished up.

Mitchell Moore was a baby boomer who made white T-shirts and Dickies his signature look. At first glance, people thought he was a contractor. His inquisitive manner and amiable disposition quickly engaged customers into discussing their needs, and by the time they put two and two together, he won their loyalty. It wasn't unusual to encounter repeat customers in the store; Mitchell was like your crazy, paint-splattered uncle.

Mitchell switched off the paint mixer. "Hey, Madison," he said. "Haven't seen you in here for a while. I thought I lost one of my regulars. What are you working on now?"

"I'm between projects," I said. I turned my back on the paint swatches. Alongside of the rack of brands that were carried at the big box decorating firms was a stack of empty cans featuring the colors I endorsed. "How are sales of the Mad for Mod paints?"

"Not gonna lie. Things slowed up when you went out of business."

"Is that what you think? That I closed shop?"

He shrugged. "Business all over town have been hit hard. I read about your trouble in the paper, so I wasn't surprised."

I could tell he meant it. Mitchell wasn't angry or sad about my problems. He accepted them as a natural ending to a sentence. For some reason, everybody accepted it. Everybody but me.

"You in the market for some tray liners?" he asked.

Tray liners. Less than a dollar a piece. Even if I were in the market, Mitchell wasn't going to get rich off me. All of a sudden, the effort it took to keep denying I was in trouble was too much.

"I need work," I said. "I haven't gone out of business, but I'm not in business either. My storefront is empty, so I'm not attracting clients, and if I don't get a client, I won't have money to invest in inventory. Every bank I went to rejected my loan application. I enrolled in business school, but"—I paused, unsure how much of the truth I should share—"there are issues with that too."

He tipped his head back and scratched his chin. 'I could give you a couple hours around here, but I can't say it's a long-term solution," he said.

I quickly waved his offer away. "I appreciate the offer, but I'm not going to tax your business to get capital to spend on mine. I was thinking—hoping—you might have an idea for another endorsement deal?"

"Hate to say it, but you'll need to make yourself a hot commodity first." He waved toward the paint cans. "A year ago, I couldn't keep these in stock. Now they're collecting dust."

"A year ago," I repeated. "That's just about the time we renovated my apartment building. Seems like longer."

"Yep. Last October. I would have thought the income from the rent on that building would keep you afloat."

"Afloat, yes. Flush, no." I cocked my head and looked at a chalkboard on the back counter of Mitchell's wrap stand. "What's that?" I pointed.

"Home decorating courses. A local trade school asked me to speak to one of their classes, and I got the idea to run weekend classes here. Now I hold workshops in the shed out back. Max capacity is twenty, but it'll do."

"That's a good idea."

"You know how it is, Madison. When you're in business for yourself, you see ideas everywhere."

18

MITCHELL WAS RIGHT. I USED TO SEE IDEAS EVERYWHERE. MY problem wasn't with funding. It was with picking a direction. One legal setback had made me afraid to charge forward and take chances. It left me stuck in a rut. I needed to do something, to decorate something. Anything. I needed to put my mind and my hands to work, to start and complete a project for no reason other than I could.

"I don't know why you're wasting your time in business school. You already know how to run a business. Check out the workshops. Expanding your skill set seems like the better investment."

I approached the chalkboard and scanned the list of classes. They covered upholstery, laying tile, installing hardwood floors, and updating kitchen cabinets. They were targeted to the DIY home warrior, not the sort to hire out a decorator, but wouldn't a decorator be an even better decorator if she brushed up on her ability to do this stuff herself?

"No, I don't need any paint tray liners," I said. Mitchell's smile faltered. "But I will need supplies to strip paint off walls.

I've been meaning to do something with the sitting room inside my house, and I suspect there's original knotty pine under a couple coats of Navajo White. And if I'm going to refinish the walls, I might as well redo the whole room. That means pulling up the carpet and refinishing the hardwood. You have a course on that, right?"

Mitchell's smile returned. "The carts are behind you."

I loaded up on liquid paint strippers, brushes, gloves, and —despite what I'd said—paint tray liners, which would make the task easier to manage, added in detergent, some buckets, two dozen sponges, and wood cleaner. I spent forty-five minutes drooling over wood stain and then, on Mitchell's suggestion, went with a pre-stain and a water-based polyurethane sealer to allow the natural grain to shine. I could already see what I wanted the finished project to look like: warm, pine walls, a nubby tweed teal sofa, and floor-to-ceiling bookcases to showcase vintage books and knick-knacks. A starburst clock and an entertainment console that housed record albums and a stereo. Astronaut den meets airplane lounge. So much of atomic mid-century design had been influenced by the space race and I could do an homage. For the first time in a long time, I couldn't wait to get started.

I paid for my supplies. All this time, I'd been thinking I had nothing to work with. I'd been so focused on what I didn't have that I hadn't stopped to see what I did.

Rocky and I headed home. I changed out of my shirtwaist dress and into a threadbare blue pinpoint cotton oxford once owned by Tony Yanuzzi, a high school teacher in the Dallas public school system from 1963 to 1988. His wardrobe consisted of button-down collar shirts, checked sport coats, and at least twelve pair of Bass loafers. The shirts were two sizes too big but made perfect paint smocks for times like these. The rest of his wardrobe sat sealed in boxes in my attic.

The temperature was in the eighties, and the air was still. I went into the storm cellar and retrieved a stack of plastic shower curtains printed with giant green daisies to use as drop cloths and a baby gate to keep Rocky from interfering with the project. When I climbed up, I stood still for a moment and watched Rocky chase a butterfly. He might make the painting process more difficult, but I didn't have the heart to make him go inside when he'd had so few hours to rollick in the yard lately.

Before I started the project, I called Joanie Higa, one of two close friends I'd made thanks to Mad for Mod. The other, Connie Duncan, was in the process of opening a flower shop. Two weeks ago, she left for the annual landscape show in Orlando and, according to the postcard I received, had extended her stay.

Joanie owned Joanie Loves Tchotchkes, a local thrift store that occasionally beat me to the punch on trash day. We'd bonded over a carton of record albums at Canton First Trade days and had been buying and selling boxes of inventory to each other ever since.

"I'm redoing my sitting room," I said after hello. "Stripping the paint, recovering the sofa, installing bookcases. You wouldn't happen to still have that collection of vintage scientific manuals that's been collecting dust on your bookshelves, would you?" The phone was silent. "Hello? Joanie? Are you there?" I clicked the receiver a few times. This was the hazard of keeping a seventies donut phone in use.

"Madison?" Joanie's voice squawked.

"Joanie?"

"You're working on a project?"

"I've been meaning to do something with the front sitting room, the room right off the main entrance. I barely use it since it's like having two living rooms, but maybe now's the time to tackle it. Get back into the flow of things before I reopen the studio."

"Your studio on Greenville Ave?"

"Yes. Why are you repeating everything I say? Is this a bad connection?"

"Where are you?"

"I'm at home," I said. "I'm about to mix up the paint stripper."

"Do you want some help?"

"I won't turn it down."

"I'm on my way." She hung up before I had a chance to question her motivation.

I brewed a fresh pot of coffee for the two of us and pulled a nut roll out of the freezer to thaw then pulled on a pair of yellow rubber gloves and poured paint stripper into a paint tray. I spent the hour until Joanie arrived focusing solely on the walls. I painted on the stripper in thick batches over two-foot square sections at a time and then moved on, letting the chemicals do most of the heavy lifting.

Rocky took off to the front door, and soon Joanie let herself in. She carried a cardboard box that she dumped on the kitchen floor.

Joanie was a petite Japanese American with rockabilly style. She had long jet-black hair she wore in an Ann Margret-inspired style with red lipstick and black winged eyeliner. After a brief affair with bowling shoes while she recovered from a twisted ankle, she was back to her usual attire of beauty smock, skinny jeans, and stilettos. I was surprised she'd returned to the stilettos after twisting her ankle, but between her hair and her shoes, she added six inches to her height.

"I would have come to your store for those," I said.

"These are from my private collection. I let my assistant run the store today. You gave me an excuse to not sit around eating cheese puffs, so you get first pick." She kicked her shoes off next to the storm cellar doors and set the box on the floor of my living room. "I'm surprised Tex didn't offer to help you."

"Tex can't be seen over here. We have to pretend we don't know each other."

"I thought you guys came out of the closet."

"We did. And then I enrolled in business school, and my professor was murdered, and now Tex is undercover at the college."

"It's great how you two work together."

"This wasn't something I wanted," I said. "It's put a strain on us."

Joanie left the cart of books in my living room and joined me. "How come? If he's undercover, he must be thrilled he can count on you to back up his story. What's his cover, anyway?"

"Rex Allen, hat store owner. Sells Stetsons."

She burst out laughing. "That's hilarious. You've got him watching Doris Day movies, and it spilled into his police work. How did he tell you?"

"He didn't exactly tell me. He told the class while I was there."

"I hope you kept a straight face," she said. "But I was right. He *definitely* needs you to get people to believe him."

Joanie would have been right if the plan had been something Tex and I had agreed upon first, but that was not how it unfolded. I wasn't yet ready to talk about how we'd left things last night. Tex and I had always been two independent operators, and this was no different. But somehow, we'd also always been able to work in tandem. We had a synergy I never could have predicted; even when we came at a problem from opposite sides, we ended up meeting in the middle (sometimes by accident). This was the first time he'd gone undercover in an investigation since I met him, and I wasn't sure I liked how it felt.

Joanie assessed the walls. "What's the vision?" she asked.

"I'm calling it the 'Glenn Den'," I said. "Part astronaut, part crash pad. Refinish the knotty pine walls, expose the hardwood, and install floor-to-ceiling bookcases. Put a media console over here"—I gestured to the north wall—"and a tweed sofa over here." I gestured to the opposite side of the room.

"Lighting?"

"Globe lamps, or something that looks like planets."

She pulled a pair of leather work gloves out of her back pocket and pulled them on. "Where do I start?"

WORK, as I'd anticipated, was the perfect antidote to my busy mind. First, we emptied the room of furniture, which proved a challenge for two middle-aged women. Eventually we triumphed. Joanie mixed two batches of paint stripper, and we took turns on opposite walls of the room. Once the stripper was applied, we gave it thirty minutes to bubble up and then scraped the residue off easily with wide plastic scrapers that kept the wood intact. When the majority of the paint was gone, we were left with the nasty task of getting it out of corner seams and ceiling joints.

I filled a bucket with warm, soapy water, grabbed a couple of sponges, and returned to find Joanie on my front steps playing catch with Rocky. I let them be and wiped the residual paint off the entire room to prepare for sanding and conditioning. While the surface air-dried, the three of us went to the kitchen for a well-earned break. Two of us had coffee and nut roll, and one of us had water and kibble.

Emboldened by the endorphins physical labor provided, I confided in Joanie. "Tex is mad at me," I said. I reached for the note he gave me last night and handed it to her. "I can't tell if we're on a break while he's conducting this investigation. Are we free agents?"

"Do you want to be a free agent?"

"No. I'm ready. I'm in. Except..." I picked at my nut roll. "Tex may have overheard something that made it seem as though I'm going on a date tonight."

Joanie picked up her coffee cup and peered inside. "Is this coffee spiked?"

"It's the dean of the business school. I told him I might end up dropping out, and he asked me to have dinner with him. And Tex walked in on the tail end of the conversation, so he didn't hear the dropping-out part."

"That sounds like a date, all right."

"Except..."

"You have got to stop doing that."

"The dean said he wanted to discuss a decorating dilemma. He said he needed someone like me, and truthfully, I need a client. Right now, I'm stuck in a loop where I can't get clients without inventory and I can't get inventory without clients. And don't even get me started on the banks."

"Are you sure you're thinking about your decorating business?" she asked. She wrapped her hands around her coffee mug and studied me. "You're not dumb. You know this might be a date, and you know how that's going to make Tex feel." She took a sip of her coffee and set down the mug. "You're stirring up trouble, and a part of you knows it. I just hope you're prepared for the fallout."

19

JOANIE AND I FINISHED OUR BREAK AND RETURNED TO THE sitting room. Rocky sat in his bed in the living room and watched us. The walls were dry, and we each took two walls and worked on conditioning the newly stripped wood. The knots in the pine darkened with the application of the product, and I was tempted to skip the sealing process. This was turning out better than I expected.

I directed Joanie to the storm cellar for fans to help circulate the air and expedite drying. Rocky, ever the useful assistant, followed her.

Despite the open windows, I needed fresh air. I went out the front door and down the steps then walked to the sidewalk and approached the building next door. It was still for sale. It was going to be a hard sell for Dennis, and the asking price wasn't enough to put it at the top of his priority list. I still had a chance at it but not if I waited too long.

I pressed my nose up against the glass and peered inside. Something moved along the far wall. I unrolled the sleeve of my shirt and wiped the glass clean and then looked again. The gray cat was inside. It looked directly at me and meowed. I couldn't hear the sound, but I saw its mouth move. How had it gotten in there?

I went to the front and checked the door, but it was locked. The back door was locked too. The cat, startled by the sounds, froze, and then limped away to a pile of boxes. My heart broke a little as I realized the cat was hurt. I went home and called Dennis.

"Dennis, this is Madison. I'm calling about the building next to my property."

"Has something changed with your situation?"

"Not mine. The cat. It's trapped inside, and I think it's hurt."

Dennis cursed. "I showed the place yesterday and that cat must have snuck inside. I'm at an offsite meeting and can't get there until tomorrow."

"You can't leave it there with no food or water," I said. "That's inhumane. Can you ask someone from your office to handle it?"

"We're all offsite."

"I could let it out if you give me the lock box code," I said. "I'm a former client, a local business owner, and a personal friend. You can trust me."

After a brief pause, he gave me the code. "Remember to lock up when you leave."

I went back to the building and let myself in. The simple act of walking up to the front door and then using the key from the lockbox felt familiar in a future sense, as though this was something I'd do again and again and again.

I entered and propped the door open behind me then made kissy noises and called out to the cat. "Hey, kitty, it's okay. I'm going to get you help." I spotted a gray tail sticking out from behind a stack of boxes at the back. "Hey, kitty, it's okay." I rounded the corner and saw the cat. It let out a long howl.

"Madison?" Joanie called from the doorway. Rocky stood by her feet.

I turned my head and held my finger in front of my lips. "There's a cat," I said in a low voice. "It's hurt."

Joanie slipped off her heels and crept closer. The cat looked at her and then back at me and let out another long yowl. It stood up and walked a few feet away, favoring its hind leg.

Joanie gasped. "Its leg is broken."

"That had to have just happened. I saw this cat a few days ago, and it wasn't injured. It needs to see a vet."

Joanie immediately unbuttoned her white beauty smock and revealed a T-shirt underneath. "Wrap it in this."

I eased myself around the boxes and held out my hand for the cat to sniff. It seemed to recognize we were there to help. I bent down and lifted it, and discovered, unintentionally, it was female. Joanie held her smock out and swaddled the cat while I held her and then cradled her quivering body to my shirt.

"Rocky's vet is on East Grand Avenue," I said. "Can you drive?"

"Yep." She scooped up Rocky. "Let's go."

***

IT WAS after seven by the time Joanie dropped me back off at home. She agreed to keep Rocky for the evening. The cat was still with the vet, recovering from emergency surgery on her broken hind leg. I think we both would have waited there all night if the veterinarian staff had permitted.

I'd agreed to meet the dean for dinner, a date I still planned to keep. If there was one thing I needed, it was a client.

Plus, he could fill in some gaps about Professor Gallagher.

The chemical smell had largely dissipated from the sitting room, but we'd left a mess. I collected all the used paint-stripping supplies and threw them into a reinforced plastic garbage bag and carried it outside. I gathered up the plastic shower curtains and threw them out too. I double-checked that the building next door was properly locked and then returned home. A quick shower eradicated any lingering scents and a slap and dash of makeup and mousse made me date-ready.

I dressed in a green silk sheath dress and matching jacket lined in white with green polka dots, sheer hose, and black patent kitten heel pumps. Even a one-inch heel threw off my gait, but Keds felt like the wrong choice for an evening business meeting over dinner. The outfit originally belonged to Moira Graham, the namesake behind Moira Graham's School of Dance. Her estate included four dozen leotards, soft leather ballet shoes, and Capezio jazz oxfords. Sadly for me, her feet were two sizes bigger than mine, so the footwear went to a home via one quick eBay transaction. I transferred my necessities into a small black clutch handbag and left.

I parked in the lot and walked to Canfield. The campus was empty. After a few minutes waiting in front of the building I entered and found the dean in Room 102 sitting behind the desk.

"Madison, lovely to see you." He stood and assessed my outfit. "And you are looking lovely."

"Thank you," I said. "A client dinner is always a good excuse to get dressed up."

"A client—oh, yes, of course." He picked up his briefcase. "I took the liberty of reserving a table at a local restaurant. It's just on the other side of the campus, so we can leave our cars here and walk."

"Sounds good."

We walked side by side toward the front door. He held up his briefcase. "Do you mind waiting here while I lock up my class notes? I'd rather not look so professorial when we walk in." He smiled politely, and after I nodded, left me in the lobby.

I wandered to the display cases and stared at the picture of Donna Nast. There was something impressive about the way she took control of her life and ran with it. Her fierce independence wasn't dissimilar to how I'd once felt.

My thoughts about Nasty were interrupted by my phone. I pulled it out of my handbag and saw Tex's name on my screen. I glanced to my left and right and then answered in a hushed voice. "Hey," I said. "I can't talk long."

"Me neither," he said. "Listen, Night, about tonight."

"It's a client meeting, that's all," I said. "We're going to a local restaurant for dinner and then I'm going home. I'll probably be in bed by nine thirty."

"What's the restaurant name?"

"I don't know. He said it was just on the other side of the campus. We're walking."

"Don't go," he said.

"Why not?" I asked. "Is Hugo a suspect?"

"He's not at the top of my list."

"Then what? This can't be about jealousy. Your life before us was far more sordid than mine."

"I can't get into it now. Just make up an excuse and cancel."

I sensed movement in the hallway, and I turned. Hugo was headed my way. "This is a business dinner," I said. "You have your business, and I have mine. Trust me, Tex. There's nothing to worry about." I disconnected and dropped my phone into the pocket of my dinner coat.

"All set. Shall we?" the dean asked. He bent his arm and held his elbow toward me as if expecting me to loop my arm through it.

Oh, no. Maybe this was a date after all?

I pretended to search my pockets for my phone and then pretended I couldn't get my handbag open. I pretended my hands were cold, and I jammed them into the pockets of my coat. I pretended Tex hadn't been right.

Hugo recovered quickly. He put his hands in his pants pockets and walked alongside me. His gait was different than most men, thanks to his cowboy boots. While we walked, he talked about campus politics (he was pro-student body government but anti-faculty union), his tastes in music (he liked tribal music from non-Western cultures), and his affinity for western wear (he owned twelve pairs of cowboy boots). He didn't seem interested in my opinions on any of the subjects. Nor did he seem interested in bringing up his decorating dilemma.

As soon as I saw the sign above the restaurant, I knew it was familiar. Kanin's, it proclaimed in white neon. It took a moment to remember where I'd seen it before: on Eric's flyer, which was still in my backpack. There was a special event tonight, but I couldn't remember what it was.

Kanin's was bustling. A group of students stood outside. At closer glance, I recognized several from the business school. The men had traded college sweatshirts and jeans for sport coats, shirts, and ties. The women had traded their collegiate attire for dresses more revealing than the September temperature demanded. Ah, youth.

Eric separated himself from the crowd and came over. "Hey, Dean," he said jovially. He glanced at me and then did a double take. "Madison. You weren't in class tonight."

"I'm not sure I'm cut out for business school."

"Are you going to work for one of the big firms like I suggested?"

"I'm still considering my options."

"I'll bet you are." He turned back to the dean. "Your table is up front like you requested."

"Great. Thank you, Eric. Madison? Are you ready to go inside?"

"Sure," I said hesitantly. This felt less and less like a business meeting, and as much as I didn't like Tex telling me what to do, I felt a pang of guilt. How was I to have known? "Can you give me a moment? I'm waiting for a phone call from the vet."

"Dog?"

"Cat." I pointed at the door. "Go on inside. I'll join you in a moment."

I waited until he was through the doorway to call Tex back. The call went to voicemail. "It's Madison," I said. "I need to apologize. You were right. I'm going to cut the evening short. I can't get into it now, but I'll explain everything when I talk to you later." I paused. "I hope your night goes better than mine."

I slipped my phone back into my handbag and went inside. The hostess directed me to the coat check, where I handed over my satin coat. There were only so many delays I could invent before being seated, and I'd worn out more than half of them.

Being with the dean of the business school, even on a platonic level, got attention. He was affable with the students, and none seemed to mind his presence. I was escorted to his table in the center of the restaurant. There appeared to be a floor show, since all seats were aimed in the direction of the stage.

Hugo helped me into my chair. I set my handbag to the left of the salad plate and scanned the room for other familiar faces.

And found one sitting next to a buxom blonde in a low-cut black jersey dress: Tex. And judging from the expression on his face, he hadn't gotten my message.

2 0

THERE WAS NO PRETENDING TEX AND I DIDN'T SEE EACH OTHER. I cocked my head and smiled at him in a *Busted!* manner and followed it up with a finger-wiggle wave. Dean noticed and grinned. "Is that Rex Allen? Well, what do you know? Eric outdid himself."

"What did Eric do?" I asked.

"Eric's an event planner. He puts together talent showcases at college-adjacent restaurants. I suggested he may want to expand his promotional reach to outside the campus. Tonight is Bongo Night." He leaned forward. "Do you like African rhythms, Madison? They drive me *wild.*" He drummed the table with his fingertips and grinned.

I pressed my lips together in the closest I could come to a smile, and I leaned back and looked at Tex. He had his arms stretched out along the back of his booth. His date was eating a shrimp cocktail. Tex raised his glass in an across-the-room toast, and I realized I did not yet have a drink to toast back. "You know, I think we should invite Rex and his date to join us. Don't you?" I said to the dean. "It seems a shame to make

148

them watch from the side of the room when we have two vacant seats right here."

I couldn't tell whether Dean had gotten the message about my lack of interest in him or if he had shifted his area of interest to Tex's date (who had two very pronounced areas of interest), but either way, he agreed. He stood up and gestured to them to join us. Tex looked surprised at first but then whispered to the blonde. She looked at us too. She finished off her last shrimp, and then they eased out of their booth and crossed the room.

"Dean Wallace, Madison, this is Virginia."

"Hi, Virginia," I said.

"Pleasure to meet you," Dean said. He held out his hand and then sandwiched hers between his. "Call me Hugo"

"Charmed, I'm sure," Virginia said. Her voice was low, and her accent was full-on Texan, and the words came out like velvet dipped in honey.

If there had been any doubts about the dean's interest in me versus her, they were certainly clear now. I crossed my arms and looked at Tex. *What did I tell you?* my body language said.

Virginia sat opposite me, and Tex sat opposite the dean. This allowed for conversations between fake couples and real couples but wasn't good for girl talk. For all the familiar faces around the room, I'd never seen Virginia before, and unless she was a new recruit, she didn't work for the Lakewood Police Department.

A waiter came by to take our drink order. "Can we get some dinner menus as well?" I asked.

"The kitchen is closed, ma'am. I can probably get you a shrimp cocktail."

"That was what I did," Virginia said. She giggled.

"Then two shrimp cocktails, please," I said.

"I'm not hungry," Hugo said.

"They're both for me."

The waiter listened as we ordered our drinks. After he left, I pushed my chair back. "I'll be right back. Powder room," I added as an explanation.

I left the room as a burst of Afro-Cuban music exploded from the stage. As soon as I was past the crowd of onlookers stationed at the back of the room, I went to the bar and flagged down our waiter. "I'd like to change my drink order to club soda, please, but I'd rather no one at the table knows. Put it on this." I opened my wallet and held out a credit card.

"You got it." He took my card and ran it through the card reader then filed it in a small box to the side of the register. It wasn't the most secure system in the world, but I had bigger fish to fry.

I went outside and called Joanie. "How's your date?" she asked.

"I'm not on a date, but Tex is."

"Madison, stop being so jealous. Tex isn't on a date."

"Yes, he is. He's at the same club as me, and he has a date. And she looks exactly like the kind of woman you would expect Tex to date."

"I don't want to sound judgmental, but considering you two have been together for over six months, aren't *you* the kind of woman Tex would date?"

"That's not what I mean."

"Besides, is Tex on a date, or is *Rex* on a date?"

She had a good point. "Have you heard from the vet about the cat?"

"It's still touch and go."

"Keep me posted." I said goodnight and hung up.

Back inside the club, the music was in full force. Hugo and Virginia were on the dance floor. Two shrimp cocktails sat at my place setting. Tex leaned back. "Everything okay?" he asked.

"That remains to be seen."

"I told you not to come," he said.

"And I told you this wasn't a date. You could have done me the favor of reassuring me as well."

"This *is* a date," he said. "For Rex," he added. "Rex and Virginia are close." He held up his hand with his fingers crossed. "Like this."

"It doesn't look that way to me." I pointed at the dance floor, where Hugo and Virginia were challenging Tex's definition of close. He shrugged. "She's a free spirit."

"She doesn't look free to me."

Tex leaned forward. "If I didn't know any better, I'd say you were jealous."

I could deny it, but I'd be lying.

I had notoriously sworn off relationships when I moved to Texas. A traumatic breakup led to the move, and the fallout came back to haunt me a few years later. The safer move seemed to keep up my guard and focus on my business.

But walls came down, and cold hearts melted. I found myself torn between two men and made the safe choice, which didn't last. Turns out I was more of a risk-taker than I thought. I resisted the impractical attraction to Tex as long as I could. The circumstances surrounding the college put a new twist on things. At least one thing was certain; life with Tex wasn't boring.

The waiter arrived with a fresh tray of drinks. He set mine down first and then a champagne flute for Virginia and two glasses for Tex and the dean. "What are you drinking?" I asked.

"Vodka and soda. How about you?"

"Same." I raised my glass of club soda. "Cheers," I said. He raised his glass and clinked. Tex emptied half of his glass on the first swig. He was a beer drinker and drank in moderation. I'd never seen him drunk. He stared at my glass, and I took another sip and smiled.

Tex surprised me with his ability to hold his liquor. He grew quiet as the night went on, not bothering with small talk to any of us. Hugo, on the other hand, was the life of the party. He spent much of the night dancing with Virginia, who seemed to have a built-in motor in her hips. At one point the dean joined the band and took over on the Conga drum. I learned a lot about Hugo; sadly, none of it had to do with a decorating opportunity.

I finally excused myself and went to find the bathroom. The line moved extra slowly, and I distracted myself with people watching. In this part of the restaurant, the back of the room and hanging around the bar, a college crowd collected. I hadn't thought much about it, but the tables where we'd sat hadn't been populated with students. Eric's event planning had certainly packed the place, but he seemed to have lucked out with the dinner crowd lingering for the floor show.

I spotted him talking to the bartender. The two chatted briefly, and the bartender gestured toward the box with the credit cards. Eric seemed nervous. He glanced over his shoulder twice while the two of them spoke and then nodded. His shoulders relaxed, and he left the bar. I'd have to remember to congratulate him on the success of his event, even if he hadn't wanted me to know it was taking place.

That in itself seemed odd. He'd given Tex a flyer in class.

Why hadn't he given one to me? Was it part of the bro code, or was I simply not his desired demographic? An astute businessperson would know not to prescreen potential attendees from an event. It wasn't like there was a bouncer or a red carpet, and it wasn't like I was riffraff. Eric had been comfortable attacking my business in class, and the idea of challenging him about his in front of his peers was almost satisfying enough to make me rethink dropping the course.

I was next in line to enter the restroom when the door swung open and a brunette came out. "Watch out in there," she said. "Somebody made a mess." She stumbled past me and went directly to the bar.

I pushed the door in and peered around the corner. Toilet paper was strewn across the wet floor, and a pair of feet in high-heeled boots jutted out from under one of the stalls. The sound of retching came from the stall, and my stomach clenched in response. My bladder was about to burst, but I tapped on the door instead. "Are you okay in there?"

The retching was replaced with sobs. I tried the door, but it was locked from inside. I shifted my weight from foot to foot and called out again. "Can I get you anything?"

The woman inside coughed and then hiccupped. The toilet flushed, and her feet retracted, and a few minutes later the door opened. It was Faye Talbot, the tall blonde who had dropped out of Radical Business Strategy.

2 1

Faye was not looking her best. Her hair was pulled into a severe ponytail, her face was pale, and blue veins were visible by her temples. Her eyes were bloodshot, and dark circles showed underneath. Her peachy-pink lipstick was smeared below her lower lip. She immediately bent down over the sink and rinsed out her mouth and then splashed water on her face. She reached for a paper towel, but the dispenser was empty.

"Great," she said.

I went into the neighboring stall and pulled several tissue seat covers from the dispenser and then handed them to her. "Here," I said. "This will be better than toilet paper."

She blotted her face. A faint transfer of makeup showed on the tissue. She balled it up and set it on top of the overflowing trash. "I need to get out of here," she said.

There's a bonding ritual that takes place in ladies' restrooms in restaurants, bars, and clubs across America. It's the girl code, an unspoken understanding that we have one another's backs. There were three people at my table, and two

154

of them wouldn't miss me. The third, well, I'd explain everything to him later.

"I'll walk you home," I said. "Just give me a minute to pee."

We went from restroom to exit as soon as I finished washing my hands. I held onto Faye's hand and led her through the crowd, not paying much mind to the curiosity and attention two blondes of varying generations negotiating a crowd of college students could attract. We reached the door, and Faye pushed past me and dry heaved over a plant to the left of the entrance. Good thing they already had a crowd; Faye's actions might deter potential patrons.

Faye lived in student housing on the opposite side of the campus. The temperature had dropped, and my arms were cold. I wrapped my hands around myself and rubbed my bare arms. Faye had her arms pressed against her sides with her fists balled up.

"My car is in Lot B," I said. "I know your apartment is close, but it'll be warmer."

"No," she said. "I don't want to go into that parking structure. That's where—" She stopped talking abruptly and put her hand up over her mouth. I steered her toward a row of bushes and held her hair back, but it seemed she was finally empty.

When she stood up, she looked like she'd lost ten pounds since we left the restaurant. Her cheeks were sunken and her lips, now devoid of lipstick, were so pale they almost matched her face. This didn't appear to be a case of overindulgence on her part.

Faye didn't seem in the mood to talk. She didn't seem to be in the mood to walk either. "My car is right inside," I said. "I think you should sit down."

"No," she protested. "I won't go there." For someone as weak as she was, her conviction was strong.

By now, news of Professor Gallagher's death had spread around the campus. Initial rumors of suicide might have died out or, in less sensitive groups, turned to inappropriate jokes at his expense, but instead, the contrasting accounts of what had happened to him had spawned conspiracy theories. I was among a handful of people who knew the truth, but attempting to correct the record would have compromised the investigation. I didn't like to see Faye struggle with her issues, but my loyalties were with Tex.

I held onto Faye's hand for the rest of the walk, though it was more like she held onto mine. Her hand gripped mine like a child who was still learning to walk. We crossed the quad, varying the straight line between point A to point B so we could benefit from the exterior lights. About two thirds of the way there, a campus police golf cart pulled up behind us.

"Can I give you a ride home?" the officer asked.

My feet had just about had it with the pointy-toed kitten heels, and the golf cart looked welcoming. "Faye, I know we're close, but I think we should take him up on his offer," I said.

"Okay," she said. She climbed in next to him, and I wedged myself in next to her. There was space for two, so I clung to the rollbar and prayed we'd steer clear of any golf-cart hazards.

The officer followed Faye's directions to her building, and I let her out. I started to see her to her door, and she protested. "I'm okay now," she said. "I don't need any more help, not from you, not from anybody. Just leave me alone. All of you!"

She turned around and stormed into her building, leaving me (and my jaw) on the stairs.

I still waited until she had the door unlocked and was safely inside before I left. I descended her stairs and bent down to look at the campus police officer.

"Was she your daughter?" he asked.

"No, just someone who looked like she needed help." I found myself at the end of the needed-help equation. "I know you're not a taxi service, but is there any chance you can give me a ride to my car in Lot B?"

"Hop in."

The ride back to the garage should have been more pleasant what with both of my butt cheeks on the seat, but I couldn't shake Faye's emotional about-face. She'd been sicker than sick at the restaurant, then pale and frail, and then sullen. The angry outburst had come out of nowhere, as had the energy to storm away from me. It was almost as if the entire evening had been an act.

"You must be busy these days," I said to the CP. "After what happened in the parking structure."

"You heard about that?" he asked. I realized he didn't know I was a student at the college, and there seemed no point in telling him. "You'd think people would stay out of the parking structures, but they're like a magnet for crime."

"How so?"

He slowed the cart to pass over a speed bump. "Last year, Lot B was home base for a couple of students who dealt drugs. Two months ago, we started finding condoms in the stair-wells. A girl who looks an awful lot like your friend there"— he tipped his head backward and then continued—"said she was assaulted by a professor."

"Someone like her, or her?" I asked.

"Hard to tell. Lots of blondes on campus. They're inter-changeable." He glanced at my hair. "No offense."

"None taken." We slowed to go over another speed bump. "What happened to her?"

"The college dismissed her claims. Said there was no evidence. Another student came forward and said he saw her get into the professor's car, so her complaint lost credibility. That happens too. Students get upset about a grade and go after the professor's reputation. For the ones who can't tell their parents they're failing, that seems like the best option."

"That's not an option. That's diversion. And it's cruel."

"Defamation of character, you could argue," he said. He glanced at me and smiled. "I'm pre-law."

My head was swimming with information by the time we pulled into Lot B. I was happy to have solicited a ride from the campus police, especially after what he told me about the parking structure. I was also certain I had a surprising new lead for Tex.

My car was the lone one in the lot. The officer pulled the golf cart up to the driver's side, and I climbed out. "I feel like I should tip you."

He waved me off. "All part of my job."

I thanked him again and unlocked my car. The interior was cooler than I expected, and I shivered. I started the car, and it stalled. I tried again, and again, it stalled. The third time, it sputtered, and then there was a *bang!,* and then the engine leveled out. I left the engine running to warm up the car and climbed out. The CP parked his golf cart and met me behind the car, where we stood side by side and stared at a dirty clump of something that sat about a foot away from my car.

"Was that jammed into my exhaust pipe?" I asked.

"Yep. The bang you heard was your tailpipe exploding." He bent down and picked the blockage up.

"Don't touch that," I said. "It's evidence."

He held out his hand. "It's a wad of cheap brown paper towels," he said. "If this is a clue, then every restaurant, gas station, and bar in a ten-mile radius is a suspect." He carried the ball of paper to the trash can and tossed it inside. "This looks like a prank. Word got out about the professor's car, and somebody saw your car sitting here and thought it would be funny to try it. Sick mind, but this is a college campus. It's not the worst prank I've seen."

"A prank?" I asked. "A man was murdered in this very parking structure, and the same technique was used. If you won't call the police, then I will." I pulled my phone out of my handbag and opened my favorites. Tex would want to know about this.

Except I couldn't call him. Especially if he was still on his date inside Kanin's. This required a 911 call and patrol officers, and if it were a prank, I'd be on record as being the one who created the scare.

I could still tell Tex. When I got home. I could call him and let him know about Faye's behavior and the story the CP relayed about the parking structure.

"Ma'am, your car appears to be running okay now. If you drive with your windows down, you'll be fine."

That was it. The professor's tailpipe had been tampered with, but the car had been broken into too. I remembered the chill I'd felt when I got inside. I left the CP and went to the passenger-side door. It was bent on the frame, just like Professor Gallagher's had been.

If this was a prank, then the suspect knew details of the original crime.

2 2

I MADE THE CALL. IT WASN'T LONG BEFORE TWO POLICE CARS arrived on the scene. The campus policeman waited with me, though he seemed none too happy about it. What had started as a courtesy turned into a police matter. I'd even had to show him my student ID to prove my car was allowed to be where it was.

Ling and Sue climbed out of the first car. "Ms. Night, are you okay?" Ling asked. She held her phone out between us, and I saw a red microphone icon on the screen. Recording our conversation now made her life easier. I knew she needed my consent to be recorded, but right now anonymity was the least of my concerns.

"Yes. No one was hurt." I walked her through what happened while Sue spoke to the CP. I relayed his assessment that this was a college prank and how, until I saw the damage to my car, I'd started to think he was right.

Ling turned away from my car and switched off her phone. "Have you spoken to the captain about this?" she asked in a low voice.

"Not yet."

"Here's the deal. Your call came in over the scanner. He might have heard it. Based on the vandalism, we need to have it taken to the impound lot so we can check it out." She looked up at the Canfield Building in front of us. "Have you been on campus all this time?"

"I was on a date," I said. There seemed no point denying it now. "It's a long story."

"I'd like to hear it some time. Where is he?"

"Probably still at Kanin's. When I left, he was about to blindfold the band and tango till dawn."

"Do you think he knows you left?"

He might not have, but Tex was another story. "I'll go see."

Ling turned to Sue and the CP. "Ms. Night needs a ride to Kanin's nightclub. I think it's best she doesn't arrive in a police car."

The CP sighed. "Hop on, lady," he said. "My chariot awaits."

Two things were obvious when I re-entered Kanin's. The real party happened after midnight, and the students had taken over the establishment. Tables had been cleared from the room to make way for an expanded dance floor, and the swarm of dancing bodies was sweaty enough to have been there awhile. Tex sat along the back wall with his arm extended around the back of Virginia's chair. She was typing on her phone. Hugo was asleep in the chair next to her. His head rested on her shoulder, and she seemed unbothered by it.

As soon as Tex saw me, he pulled his arm away from

Virginia's chair and sat up straight. It was the least Rex thing he could have done, and if anyone were watching, the jig would have been up. Lucky for Tex (and Rex), the only person who seemed interested in his actions was me.

I made my way past the throng of dancers, getting jostled on the way, and sat next to Tex. "Hello," I said. "I don't suppose my date noticed I've been gone for a few hours?"

"My date kept your date too busy to notice much more than her cleavage. Sorry it didn't work out for you two. Seemed like a nice guy."

"Yes, well, I don't think he was the one. I guess I'm back to being a free agent." Even though the interior was damp with humidity and sweat, the chill from having been outside still lingered. I should have gotten my coat from coat check when I reentered, but returning in my coat would have raised questions I didn't want to answer, at least not yet.

"Don't be too hard on your date," Tex said. "I bribed the bartender to get him drunk."

I kept my bartender negotiation to myself and turned to look at Tex. "Excuse me?"

He flashed me a grin, the gleaming-white-teeth, sparkling-blue-eyes, mischievous grin that made my heart skip a beat. "Gotta protect my investments."

I raised my eyebrows. "Did you learn that in business school, Rex?"

"Nah, I figured it out on my own." He stood up and shrugged off his sport coat then extended it to me. "You look cold."

"Is that wise? Most men loan their jackets to women they came with."

"Virginia went off the clock at midnight."

I took Tex's jacket and draped it over my shoulders. "She's not a cop, is she?" I leaned forward and looked at her.

"She works at Jumbo's. The girls miss having me around. I needed a date, and she jumped at the opportunity."

My eyes widened. Jumbo's was a topless bar across the street from the Casa Linda Shopping Center. I'd been inside exactly once. The bar had remained in business while many of the other shops and restaurants in the area had turned over, and for a moment, I recognized Jumbo's probably had a sound business model. I considered setting up a meeting with the owner to pick her brain about debt-to-income ratio and customer loyalty programs, but I wasn't sure I was that evolved.

I glanced at Virginia and then back at Tex. "By 'the girls' I assume you're talking about other dancers and not Virginia's anatomy. Correct?"

He chuckled. He leaned close to me and whispered, "Virginia's not my type." The sensation of his hot breath on my cold ear sent a different kind of shiver down my spine.

I turned to him. Our faces were close. "Oh? What's your type, Rex?"

"Well, that's the thing. My tastes run a little narrow these days. I'm a sucker for businesswomen who look like Doris Day."

I sat back. "Isn't that a coincidence. I have a business—a decorating business—and would you believe it was inspired by Doris Day?"

"What are the odds. I don't reckon you'd be interested in getting a cup of coffee with me sometime, would you?" he asked.

My heart swelled. If *Rex* asked me out, then we could be us in public. One less stressor.

"You jump, I jump, Jack," I said.

Tex's phone buzzed. "Excuse me a moment," he said. He stood up and left me with Virginia and the dean.

Flirting with Tex in public was fun, but when he found out what had happened in the parking structure, I wondered whether he'd appreciate my commitment to keeping his cover or if he'd be upset that I'd kept him out of the loop.

I shifted to the chair next to Virginia. "You're a trooper," I said. "Did you manage to have some fun while you were on the clock?"

"Are you kidding? I got business cards from four different fraternities and a couple of professors too. With the jobs I can book, I might be able to go freelance by the end of the year."

Seems like everybody had been bit by the entrepreneurial bug.

"You want some champagne?" she asked. She bent down, and a pack of male students stared, hopeful she'd have a wardrobe malfunction. She raised a bottle of Dom Perignon and held it out to me. "I lost track of my flute, so you'll have to drink it straight from the bottle."

"No, thanks," I said.

"Suit yourself." She took a swig and then propped the bottle on her thigh with her hand around the neck. "Mmm-mmm, that's good." She closed her eyes and licked her lips and then smiled.

I was an MBA student who couldn't get the bank to give me a loan against my house, and Virginia, a topless dancer from Jumbo's, was on a date with my current leading man, buying herself bottles of Dom Perignon, and swimming in business opportunities. The world felt tilted. Add in the vandalism to my car, and the night was a bust. And when Tex returned from his phone call, which I strongly suspected was from one of the two Sues, I wouldn't be better off—I'd be worse.

Something had to give.

I reached out and grabbed the bottle. Virginia relinquished it and grinned. I took a swig and let the cool bubbles run down my throat. It *was* good. It was the best pink champagne I'd ever had. It was far better than flat club soda.

I handed her the bottle. "Virginia, do you mind waiting here with the dean? I'm going to go close out at the bar."

"Sure," she said. "You could get couple of flutes if you want, but I don't think there's much left." She raised the bottle.

I went back to the bar, this time avoiding much of the dancing crowd by staying close to the wall. I had a secondary agenda, which was finding Tex and telling him what had happened. The bar was mostly empty, with the bartender at the far end, propped on his elbows, talking to the brunette I'd seen stumble out of the restroom when Faye was inside. I rested against a stool and raised my hand to get his attention.

"I'd like to close out my tab," I said.

"Sure. Name?"

"Night."

He retrieved the box of credit cards from the side of the register and flipped through tabs until he reached the Ns. "Madison?" he asked.

"Yes."

He pulled it out, unclipped an unfinished receipt, and scanned the barcode at the bottom. The register made a sound. The bartender glanced at the screen, tried to scan the receipt again, and then turned back to me. "This one's no good."

"What do you mean, it's no good?"

The bartender stepped to the side so I could see the computer screen. Across the front was one word: Rejected.

23

"Do you have another way to pay?" the bartender asked.

"That's the card I brought with me tonight. Try it again."

"I tried it twice."

"Try. It. Again."

He dutifully turned, scanned the receipt, and swiped my card. The computer made that nasty sound again. This time, under the word "Rejected," it said "Confiscate Card."

Could nothing be easy tonight?

I held out my hand. "I'll come back tomorrow and pay the tab. You can either trust me or send me to the kitchen to wash dishes. I don't care which. But I have to call the company to straighten this out, and the easiest way is for me to call the number on the back."

"Sorry, ma'am, I can't give you back that card."

"That card is *my* card, and yes, you can."

"House rules."

The longer I argued with the tattooed twenty-something, the angrier I got. Door after door had been slammed in my face, and I was tired of it. I turned away from him and

167

scanned the interior of the club for Tex. Instead of seeing him, I saw Eric coming toward us.

"Is everything okay?" he asked. He shifted his attention from me to the bartender and back to me, and I wasn't sure which one of he was talking to or how different our answers might be.

"Everything is not okay. This man won't give me my credit card. I don't know what the problem with it is, but I will straighten it out tomorrow."

The color drained from Eric's face. He looked at the bartender. "Her card came up as rejected?"

The bartender nodded. "I tried to tell her the house rules, but she won't listen."

"Madison, did you apply for any loans recently?" Eric asked.

The personal nature of the question surprised me. "Yes. How did you know?"

He seemed relieved. "When the banks run your profile to see if your debt-to-income ratio is in line, they put a temporary hold on any open balances on your cards. It'll drop off in a couple of days, but the computer probably thinks you're overextended."

"I've never heard of such a thing," I said. I turned to the bartender. "Have you?"

He shrugged. "He's the business major."

"May I have my card, please?" I held out my hand.

"I told her the policy," the bartender told Eric.

"Eric, you are smart enough to know you're better off if I come back tomorrow and pay than if you anger me and I never come back. Once I straighten this out, I'll have a choice: blame the bank, or blame the restaurant. This happened at your event, and I've seen two women so drunk they could barely walk and one man asleep alongside the dance floor. I don't recall seeing anyone checking IDs at the door, and the sheer number of people inside seems far beyond the recommended occupancy limit by the entrance. Would you like me to talk to the restaurant board? I'm sure they would be interested in what I have to say."

"Give her the card," Eric instructed the bartender.

The bartender shook his head. "You got balls, lady."

One more thing I didn't need.

I took the card and slipped it into my wallet then went to the coat check. Tex rested against the counter with my coat in his hands. "Is there anything I need to know?" he asked.

"That's a loaded question."

"Only if you were involved in a police matter earlier tonight."

"And if I was, would I have any reason to tell a classmate who owns a hat store?"

I snatched my coat from his hands. Gone was the playful attitude I'd had earlier. In its place was that same old feeling of looking out for myself. Tex was like everybody else in here: he wanted something. But his wants and my wants didn't overlap, and I was tired of hitting red lights in my journey.

"Good night, Rex," I said. "I'm going inside to tell my date it's time to leave."

"Your date is in no shape to drive."

"I'll put him in a cab."

"I'm going with you. Wait here." He left me by the coat check. If I didn't feel a moral obligation to the dean, I would have hopped into the waiting cab and left. But the twenty-dollar bill in my handbag wasn't enough to cover the drive, and my credit card was as worthless as a stick of gum.

Tex and Virginia returned with the dean between them,

his arms draped over their shoulders. I had to hand it to Virginia. She *was* a trooper.

We got outside, and they tucked Hugo into a cab. Tex gave Virginia his keys. "Take the Jeep. I'll get it tomorrow." He kissed her on the cheek and, after she walked away, he turned to me. "Do you want the middle?"

"I want my own cab."

"Slim pickings," he said. He was right. It was this cab or wait indefinitely.

I walked around to the far side of the cab and slid in next to Hugo. Tex got in on his side with the dean sandwiched between us.

The cab ride was in silence. Since neither Tex nor I knew where the dean of the business school lived, we flipped a coin to see who would lift his wallet. Tex lost, which turned out to be a loss for me, too, when I was left with the task of holding the dean while Tex extracted the wallet out of the dean's back pocket. He woke and tried to kiss me, and I turned my head to escape. His breath reeked of alcohol, and his kiss landed somewhere by my ear.

I propped Hugo upright while Tex pulled out his driver's license. Too bad I'd been so solicitous when it came to the check; Hugo was packing more credit than every bank I'd visited combined.

"We're in luck. He's in a house right off campus." He gave the address to the cab driver and tucked the wallet into Hugo's suit pocket.

"Shouldn't you put it back where you found it?" I asked.

"Do you want another kiss? For an unconscious man, he sure snapped into action when he thought you were coming on to him."

"Leave it in his jacket." I cracked the window. The night air pushed my hair away from my face. I closed my eyes and tried to relax. It had been a day of disjointed craziness, but everything had blurred together into one giant mess. The knotty pine wall restoration, the injured cat, the vet, the disastrous date, the sick student, the vandalized car, and the credit card situation. None of it had to do with the murder investigation, but somehow it all felt intertwined. So many things were out of my control. Seeing an inebriated faculty member home safely was the cherry on top of the sundae that was my Friday night.

Tex convinced the driver to help him get the dean inside his house, leaving me in charge of unlocking the doors and clearing the way. I waited in the living room while Tex located the bedroom and then asked the cabbie to help get Hugo in there. I followed them in and took off Dean's shoes, but that was the extent of the undressing. He could wake up in his clothes.

When I left the bedroom, I found Tex and the cabbie in the living room. "Can we leave?" I asked. "I'd rather not be here when he wakes up. It will certainly raise questions none of us want to answer." I glanced at the cabbie. "Maybe you do, but I sure don't."

"The last thing I need is to be found inside the dean's house with the cab running out front."

"Okay, then. Let's go."

The cabbie led the way to the door. He was down the stairs and inside the cab before I left. I stopped at the door and turned around to see if Tex was behind me. He wasn't. He was bent over the coffee table staring at something intently.

From the distance, I recognized a copy of *Rad Rage*, Professor Gallagher's book. Next to it was a stack of handwritten manuscript pages. Tex pulled a pencil out of his jacket and used the eraser end to fan the papers out across the table. He straightened up. "I'm going to be here awhile," he said. "Take the cab and go home."

It was as if he'd completely forgotten our flirtation at the club. I left the doorway and went farther inside the room. "You are Rex Allen, MBA student in an advance level business course. You showed great compassion and integrity by making sure your temporary professor got home safely, but you have no right to snoop around his house while he's passed out, especially since you admitted to bribing the bartender to get him drunk. You've already compromised yourself by asking the cab driver to assist in your good deed because now he can place you—us—inside this house."

Tex didn't lose sight of things like this, and it struck me as odd that he'd been so careless tonight. "Come look at this," he said.

It was the one response I hadn't expected. I crossed the room and looked at the title page. Sprawled across it was the title and byline *Anger Management by Hugo Wallace.*

"That's him," I said, pointing to the bedroom.

"Check the text," Tex said.

"Why me?"

"You were his date. You have a reason to be here."

I picked up the stack of pages and flipped through them. The handwriting, though sloppy, relayed familiar concepts. I picked up *Rad Rage* and paged through that too.

Tex glared at me. "What? I was his date. I have a reason to be here." Inside, the text was liberally highlighted. In the second chapter, I found a passage that was a word-for-word duplicate of the text written on the loose pages. "There are entire passages that are the same. Did Hugo ghostwrite

Gallagher's book? Or did Gallagher write it and now Hugo's plagiarizing it?"

"Theft of intellectual property is a serious charge."

"Especially in academic circles." I held *Rad Rage* up. "Remember in class when Hugo said Gallagher didn't clear his required reading? Why would he care now?"

Tex was tense. He glanced in the direction of the bedroom. "This could be motive."

"You said Hugo wasn't at the top of your list."

"He is now."

I didn't like what it meant, but if Tex was right, then I'd just been on a date with a murderer.

24

Was it possible the jovial dean of admissions to the business school was responsible for Professor Gallagher's death?

Tex pulled his phone out and took pictures of the table. He glanced around and then pointed to the door. "Let's go."

I didn't have to be told twice. We left together. Tex checked that the front door was locked, and then we descended the stairs. The cab driver was waiting for us.

"Is the meter still running?" Tex asked.

"You betcha." He seemed pleased by the unexpected delay.

Tex gave the driver his address. When I protested, he ignored me. "I'll give you my credit card. Take Ms. Night home after you drop me off and charge me for the total. Give her my card and I'll get it from her in class tomorrow."

"Tomorrow is Sunday," I said.

"You're right, it is." He glanced at the driver, and then back to me. "If you're free tomorrow, maybe we can get that cup of coffee we talked about at the club. Unless you changed your mind, in which case I can get the card in class on Monday."

"I'd love to," I said. I pulled a business card out of my handbag. "Call me any time." When I handed the card to Tex, I didn't let go right away. We sat in the backseat of a dirty cab, connected by a rectangular piece of 14 pt. glossy cardstock that advertised a business that wasn't currently in business. Mad for Mod had brought us together in the first place.

I let go of the card and in that moment, I released the demands everybody had tried to place on me. So many problems had filled my mind that I hadn't allowed space for solutions. And as soon as I let go, the weight of those problems lifted, and I felt free.

The cabbie dropped off Tex and then drove to my house. I gave him a healthy tip on Tex's card and added my twenty-dollar bill. "Thank you," I said.

"You gonna meet him for coffee?" he asked.

"I think I am."

"He's a good guy," he said. "Got an honest face too. I can always tell when somebody's hiding something, and that guy is on the level."

I stifled the urge to tell the driver the honest, on-the-level passenger had been hiding his identity as the captain of the local police!

The cabbie drove off before I got to my front door. I opened my handbag for my keys. but they weren't there. I patted my coat pockets. Empty. And then I remembered I'd left them in the ignition of my car, now in police impound. It was closing in on three o'clock in the morning. This was the day that wouldn't end.

Aside from an isolated incident before I moved in, I knew this neighborhood to be safe. That didn't make me want to sleep outside. I checked the doors and windows within reach but found myself to be a thorough and responsible homeowner. As I rounded the perimeter thinking of who I could call after two a.m. on a Saturday night—make that Sunday morning—I noticed the building next to me. It wasn't exactly a Hilton, but I knew the lockbox code. As long as I got out before anyone noticed, I could sleep there.

When people met me, they tended to think I was on the level too. My hair, vintage clothes, generally pleasant demeanor, and aura of Doris Day left behind the warm fuzzies that inspired trust. It was the reason the bank rejections had bothered me so much. The word "no" had always been temporary, a wall to be met with a different approach. That was where I was now. Facing a wall that needed a different approach.

I let myself into the small building and locked the door behind me. It took a moment for my eyes to adjust to the darkness. My cell phone flashlight helped. My phone rang. It was Tex. I switched it to silent just in case anyone could hear before answering. "Hey," I said quietly.

"Are you home?" he asked.

"Close enough."

"I don't want to talk about tonight. It's so late it's early, and I'm not going home any time soon."

"Is that why you called?"

"No. I wanted to tell you something I couldn't say earlier."

"What's that?"

"I love you," he said. His voice was low and sexy.

I didn't reply right away. It had been a long time since I'd heard those words in this context, and I wanted to savor the sound, the feeling, the unexpected warmth that blossomed inside my chest and then ballooned to fill the room.

"Don't say anything back," he added. "I just wanted you to know."

"Good night, Captain Allen," I said softly.

"Good night, Night."

We hung up, and I set an alarm. I opened a box filled with plastic garment bags, unfolded several, and laid them on the ground. Another box held a plastic bag filled with clothes. I picked up a shirt and sniffed the fabric to make sure it wasn't mildew (or something worse) and when it seemed clean, changed out of my dress and into the shirt to sleep in. I left my pantyhose on more for warmth than modesty. I emptied the rest of the bag onto the plastic garment bag and then burrowed myself underneath the pile. I wedged more garment bags under my head and closed my eyes. It was the least comfortable place I'd ever slept in my life, but the day had taken every ounce of energy out of me, and I fell asleep despite the discomfort.

Everything was stiff. My neck, my back, my shoulders, my legs. The phone alarm jolted me out of an REM cycle, and it took upwards of a minute to remember where I was and why. Sunlight streamed through the dirty windows, indicating it was later than I thought. I pushed the clothing items that had served as my cover to the side and sat up, wincing with pain in every joint in my body.

Out front, I heard a car door. That was enough to get me motivated to get going. I was either going to have to put on last night's clothes again or leave without pants. It was, admittedly, a low point.

In the daylight, I was able to see the garments I'd scattered around to make my sleeping surface. There were hundreds of shirts. Corduroy, cotton, wool, and denim. Most were embroidered with colorful flowers or western motifs. I looked down at the shirt I'd slept in. It was chalk-colored with an abstract rust and avocado-green cross-stitched pattern on the front placket. I reached my hand around back and felt as far up the shirt as I could. There was embroidery there too. Curious, I walked to one of the dirty windows and turned my back to it and then looked over my shoulder to see my reflection. It wasn't exactly a three-way mirror in a department store.

What was this stuff? I returned to my makeshift bed and scooped up piles of shirts to reveal the garment bags on the floor. Johnson's Clothiers, they said. *Johnson.* Thelma Johnson. Dennis had said this property was a storefront originally owned by Thelma Johnson's husband, Sam, but he'd never mentioned what business Sam was in.

I set the shirts on the garment bag and went to the back of the building and unsealed another box. Inside were jeans with the tags still on them. Dead stock. Entire size runs of jeans that had been sitting in this box for decades. Not only did it surprise me, it solved the problem of going home without pants.

I leaned over the box and rooted through until I found a pair close to my size. Just as I lifted my leg to put them on, I heard voices out front. "This lockbox is open. What the heck?"

And then the door swung open, and Dennis O'Hara walked in. Unfortunately, he wasn't alone.

"I CAN EXPLAIN," I SAID. I HELD MY HANDS UP IN AN I-surrender gesture. The jeans I'd been putting on fell to the floor, one foot in and one foot out. I bent down and pulled them up, buttoning the fly and rolling the too-big waistband so they stayed in place.

Dennis turned to the man with him. "Can you give us a moment?"

"Who is that?" the man asked.

I didn't wait for Dennis's answer. "Madison Night," I said. "I live in the house next door." I pointed at the wall between us.

"I'm sorry," Dennis said to him. "Can I see you outside?" he said to me.

I grabbed my dress and Tex's jacket and stepped into my kitten heel shoes and then followed Dennis outside. The man's eyes went to my feet, and he watched them as I walked past. His eyebrows were raised, but I carried myself proudly as if this were a perfectly normal outfit.

"What are you doing here?" Dennis asked.

"I was locked out of my house last night and needed a place to sleep."

"I trusted you, Madison. Do you know how bad this looks?"

I stood tall. "Do you know what's in the boxes in there?" I asked. "Inventory from Sam Johnson's store. Do you remember who bought out Thelma Johnson's estate? Me. I may not own the building, but I have a legal claim to everything in there, and considering you've been in several times and never once mentioned that to me, I'd say your actions don't look particularly good either."

He looked shocked. "You can't think I withheld that on purpose."

"I don't know what to think. You said Thelma Johnson sold the building to a store, but everything in there says Johnson Clothiers on it. Was it a turnkey transaction?"

"I don't know. The history of the building says it was owned by the Johnsons and then sold, and then after the hurricane in '83, the shop closed."

"I suggest you do a little more digging. Unless you can prove Sam Johnson's inventory was part of the sale of this building, I have a legitimate right to claim it."

I didn't realize the man was standing in the doorway listening to us. "Is that true?" the man who'd arrived with Dennis asked.

"Yes, it's true," I said. "I bought Thelma Johnson's estate. Thelma's son gave me her house after I agreed to make good on the back taxes. Dennis handled the transaction. I never thought much about this building because no one ever mentioned it. Dennis and I recently spoke about me buying it."

"That would have made sense. It was built with your house

and your freestanding garage. All told, it's a nice-sized corner plot with lots of space and a commercially zoned property." He gazed up at the flat roof. "Lots of damage, though. Not as sound as it was when it was built."

He left us and walked the perimeter of the property. I turned back to Dennis.

"Who is he?" I asked.

"He's a building inspector. We have an offer pending inspection."

"No."

"Yes."

"You have to give me time to meet with the bank. And I mean *meet* with them, not just run my numbers and get a computer to say I'm not good on paper. This property belongs with me."

He looked past me to the interior of the building. "Are you planning on squatting here indefinitely? Because that might dissuade the buyers."

"I have a better idea," I said.

I CALLED a locksmith to let me into my house. The first thing I did once I was inside was call Joanie. "How are the kids?" I asked.

"I picked the cat up from the vet this morning. Rocky has a new girlfriend. He hasn't left her side since we got home. He's sleeping next to the bed I made up for her right now."

"I want to hear all about her later, but first, I need a shower. Can you drop Rocky off this morning?"

"Sure," she said. "I'll be there in about an hour."

I showered and dressed in a white cotton tunic and yellow

stirrup pants then set up at the kitchen table and reviewed my class assignment. I couldn't focus. Last night at Kanin's had started with an awkward date but transitioned into a night to remember, starting and ending with Dean Wallace's un-dean-like behavior. Add in Faye getting sick in the restroom, my credit card coming up denied, and my car being vandalized, and it was too much. One of these things would have been enough, but five? What were the odds they were unconnected?

I opened the notebook in which I'd handwritten the draft of my essay for Decision Making for the Business Leader, flipped to a fresh page, and filled the next seven pages writing down everything I knew about the previous night. It was like recapping a dream: the more I focused on the generalities of the evening, the more details penetrated the hazy memory. I was thankful I'd stuck with club soda. Aside from the champagne I'd slugged from Virginia's bottle, I'd kept a clear head, which couldn't be said for the dean or for Faye.

I set the notebook down and called Mickey at police impound. "This is Madison Night. You towed my Alfa Romeo last night."

"Yeah, Tex's friend. I remember ya. You left your keys in the ignition."

"I realized that when I got home," I said. "You wouldn't happen to know when I can pick up my car, do you?"

"I do, but I don't think you're going to like my answer. Forensics is going to go over your car today, but the damage to your door is going to require some body work."

"I heard you can bend those doors back into shape," I said, repeating what Professor Gallagher had told me on that fateful day in the parking structure.

"Maybe you can with a new car but not these classic ones,"

he said. "You don't want to put a strain on those old door hinges. Getting it repaired will cost you your deductible, but in the long run, it's worth it. And if I remember, this is your second 1960s Alfa Romeo, right?" I confirmed. "There's a finite number of them out there. Don't press your odds by needing me to find you a third."

"I don't suppose you have anything I can borrow in the meantime?"

"I got a pick-up truck and a cherry red Mustang. Take your pick."

The plus about owning my dream car was this was an easy decision. "I'll be by for the truck in about an hour."

"Tex was right," Mickey said. "You're unpredictable."

I was at my laptop fleshing out a business proposal when Joanie arrived. When she opened the door, Rocky burst into the room and yapped like he had something to tell me. He hopped up onto his hind legs and put his paws on my thigh and waited for me to pet him. I ruffled his fur and then bent down and kissed his head. He dropped back down onto the floor and trotted over to his water bowl, slurping noisily.

Joanie stood behind my chair and looked over my shoulder at the notes on the table. She was dressed in a version of her usual uniform: white chef coat, skinny jeans cuffed two inches, and black stiletto pumps. Her hair was teased higher than usual and pinned up on the sides with the back hanging down. She looked like a cross between Amy Winehouse and Gordon Ramsay.

"What's all this?" she asked.

"Homework," I said. I closed the notebook and pushed it away.

Joanie poured herself a cup of coffee and sat down. "Twenty-four hours ago, you called me over here to strip paint off your walls, and then we rescued a cat. Today you look like you slept in a barn, and your business homework includes the word 'homicide.' Do you want to tell me what happened between then and now? Because I'm lost with a capital *L*."

I told Joanie about last night. She, as was to be expected, focused on one irrelevant detail. "Tex took a stripper from Jumbo's as his date? That's rich."

Under the afterglow of Tex's three a.m. pronouncement, the memory of last night took on a halo of equality. "She said it was a great place for leads. She had a handful of business cards. Just think about that for a moment. I can't get a loan to restart my business, and a dancer from Jumbo's goes to a club with the captain of the police and walks away with enough contacts to consider going freelance."

"Which part are you more upset by? That she got business leads or that she went with Tex?"

I waved Joanie's question away. "Tex needed a date. It was totally innocent."

"Then it's the business angle." She dropped into a chair and opened the cover of my notebook. "Radical Business Strategy" was sprawled across the top of the first page, and underneath, my name. Like I'd learned to do in grade school. Some lessons were never unlearned.

She closed the lid. "Don't beat yourself up. You're at a turning point. It'll come to you."

"What'll come to me?"

"How to reopen your business. If you want to reopen your business."

"Of course, I want to reopen my business." I jerked my thumb over my shoulder. "I have a partially completed room renovation at home. That's how much I miss decorating."

"Yeah, but you gotta wonder..." Her voice trailed off. "Never mind."

Joanie was a businesswoman too. She'd left a corporate job and cashed in her 401K to start up her store and used her vast business knowledge to write up a business plan. Joanie looked good on paper, which helped her open her doors six months after she got the idea. If she had thoughts on the matter, I wanted to hear them.

"You were going to say something. What?"

She raised her hands to her head and adjusted her bobby pins. "This isn't about money. I've seen you when you're on fire. When you want something, you make it happen. Don't just go through the motions, Madison. Your business is like a car that broke down on the side of the road. Figure out why you're stalled, and either fill up your tank or get a different car."

"Speaking of cars," I said, "Can you give me a ride to the police impound?"

2 6

Joanie drove a black Ford Mustang she acquired at a swap meet in Grand Prairie. We'd gone together, and by the time I finished negotiations on a collection of Russel Wright punch bowls in "Eclipse," she traded her Volkswagen Bug for the Mustang. She fixed the busted air conditioner by replacing the spark plugs and planned to overhaul the rest of it when she found the time, the parts, and the right person to do the work.

Mickey met us by the entrance. I got out of Joanie's car and greeted him.

"Madison, glad you got here early." He glanced at Joanie's black Ford Mustang. "Friend of yours or Uber?"

"Friend."

He bent down to the open passenger window and looked inside. "Nice ride," he said. He asked her a question about her chassis and horsepower, and to her credit, she knew the answers.

"Mickey?" I interrupted. "Do you have keys for me?"

He straightened up. "Oh. Yeah. Sure." He handed me two

sets of keys: mine and a set to a freshly washed pick-up truck. "She's gassed up and ready to go."

"Thanks. You'll let me know when I can get my car?"

"You'll either hear it from me or my cousin."

I thanked him and went in search of the truck while he leaned back down and resumed his conversation with Joanie. At this rate, they'd bond over her engine block before lunch.

Sometimes, I wondered about Tex's extended family. Until he told me he had a cousin who owned a towing company and oversaw the police impound lot, I hadn't given much thought to him being from Texas. But in moments like these, I saw how Tex's loyalty ran beyond simple cop lines. I liked that about him. I was even charmed by him hiring a topless dancer to accompany him to the club.

Love does funny things to the mind.

I still had to pay off my bar tab at Kanin's, but with the banks being closed, I didn't know if the hold on my available credit had lifted. Still, a promise was a promise, and a debt was a debt. In the interest of saving Rocky from having to sniff everything in our path, I led him to the truck, and we drove.

It was after noon. Kanin's lacked the energy of the previous night. There were a few cars parked to the far left but none in the customer spaces. I eased into a spot out front and cut the engine then turned to Rock. "This is a restaurant," I said. "You're not allowed."

He whimpered.

"Be a good dog. I'll be right back."

He dropped his head.

I couldn't do it. I couldn't leave him alone in the truck. Not after a murder had taken place in a parking structure within walking distance. The bag I had with me was my backpack, and Rocky didn't fit in there.

I got out of the truck and went around to the bed. There was a duffel bag filled with tools bungee-corded to the side. I lowered the back panel and leaned in to get it. Another car pulled into the parking structure. I glanced up and saw Eric behind the wheel. Even on a Saturday, he wore a bowtie. I suppose he was as committed to his look as I was to mine.

After our encounter last night, Eric was the last person I wanted to run into. I bent down behind the truck and tiptoed around to the passenger-side door. It was locked. Silly me, I hadn't yet seen the benefit to teaching Rocky how to release locks on a car.

I turned around and leaned against the truck door. If I could wait it out until Eric left, I'd be fine. I stepped my feet out in front of me and rested my tush on the floorboard. It was awkward at best.

I listened for sounds that Eric entered Kanin's, but what I heard instead was him ask a question. "Is the manager here?"

"He's in his office," another male voice answered.

"Does he suspect anything?"

"Are you kidding? He gave us a standing invitation to return."

I twisted and peered through the window. The second voice belonged to the bartender. I rested my foot on the floorboard and stayed low, watching them through the corner of the glass. Rocky raised his head and looked at me but then rested his head back on the seat.

I'd mistakenly thought Eric's role was to coordinate the entertainment, but perhaps he rented out the building and supplied the staff? The bartender, along with the hostess and wait staff, had all been college-aged, which didn't strike me as odd considering the club's proximity to the campus.

"Did you tally out? How'd we do?" Eric asked.

Eric's use of "we" confirmed my suspicion that Eric had partners. Curiosity took over, and I strained to hear how profitable event planning could be. Who knew, maybe once I locked down my second space, there would be a side business there for Mad for Mod?

"Half a ticket," the bartender said.

"Sweet." The men high-fived.

Half a ticket? How much was a ticket? Were they raising money to buy tickets to a concert? That didn't seem likely. This was the problem with spending my time around college students. They had a vocabulary that wasn't available to fifty-year-olds. I'd considered investing in Babbel so I could refresh my French. I wondered if they had a language course on Millennial Grad Student.

The men's body language was relaxed. Eric was the more formal of the two, in his broadcloth shirt and bowtie with dark denim jeans cuffed at the ankle, no socks, and brown oxfords. The bartender was in a black T-shirt, low-slung jeans, and running sneakers and had a dishtowel draped over his shoulder. Whatever a ticket or half a ticket was, it seemed to have exceeded their expectations.

"This place is a cash cow, man," the bartender continued. "We have an open invitation and all green lights. Now that Gallagher's out of the picture, there's nobody to stop us."

"There's one. The woman who demanded her credit card when she left, that blond lady. She's in Gallagher's class with me. She might make some noise."

"Madison Night? She won't be back. After she left, I voided her transaction. If she calls the bank, they won't even see what she's talking about. It was worth sacrificing my tip to get rid of her."

"I still say it's too risky," Eric countered. "If Gallagher caught on, then she could too. We can't take care of everybody like we did with him."

THE HAIR ON THE BACK OF MY NECK BRISTLED. ATTENDING A theme night on campus somehow put me in the same category as a man who had recently turned up dead. Suddenly the vandalism to my car felt less random. These guys were into something they shouldn't be, and while I didn't know exactly what it was they'd done, I knew it wasn't safe for me to pop up and say hello.

"What did she drink?" Eric asked.

"Club soda. She made a point of telling me no matter what anybody ordered for her, she was to get club soda."

"Did she think the dean was going to get her drunk?" Eric asked. They laughed. "What about the other guy? The one with the sexy date? She spent a lot of time talking to him."

"He paid cash."

These two must have loved that. If they were skimming from the profits, then cash was king. Tex might have known that, but he also would have known a credit card could compromise his cover story.

At that moment, Rocky barked. I'd left his window cracked

to give him air, but that also meant his bark wasn't muffled. The two men stopped talking. I dropped down out of their view but held onto the door handle. My knee screamed out in pain, but I bit my lip.

"Whose truck is that?" Eric asked.

"I don't know. Kitchen crew? Janitor?"

"There's a dog inside."

This was no good. Had I locked the door? Would they come investigate and find me crouched on the other side? Would I fit underneath the truck? Was I really contemplating crawling under a truck in the parking lot outside of a restaurant?

I leaned against the truck and pulled my phone out. I switched it to silent and sent a text: *call kanin's. ask for eric. Now.* I hit Send and hoped Tex wouldn't think I was being needy.

Within seconds, a third voice called out from inside the restaurant. "Eric, you got a call. Says it's urgent."

I turned around and peeked through the windows of the truck. Rocky saw me and came over to say hello. I craned my neck past him and watched both men go into the restaurant. I quickly moved to the driver side, started the engine, and peeled out of there.

I drove two miles and pulled into a parking lot. There was no doubt the conversation I overheard indicated guilt. I removed my credit card from my wallet and called the number on the back. I navigated the prompts until I reached a summary of my recent charges. The last one was my purchase at Paintin' Place. Unless the system hadn't updated with recent activity, the bartender told the truth. The bar tab from last night wasn't there. I put a hold on charges just to be safe and then disconnected.

I called the police station, hoping to catch Tex. Imogene answered, which I hadn't expected.

"Captain Allen has you working on a Sunday?" I asked. I knew he was understaffed with police officers but expecting a volunteer to work six days seemed unusual.

"I came in on my own. My air conditioner stopped working and I needed a place to write."

"I've heard people write at Starbucks," I offered.

"You have to get there early to get a table." She paused. "He's not here," she said. "I can transfer you to his cell—"

"That's not necessary." I could do that myself. "The last time we spoke, you mentioned doing research. You do a lot, don't you?"

"Sure," she said. "Sometimes the research is more fun than writing."

"Have you ever heard the expression 'half a ticket'?"

"As in admission to a club or money?"

"I don't know. What does it mean in terms of money? How much is a ticket?"

"A million."

"That's not possible."

"It is," she said. "It's big in the hip-hop community. I was thinking of writing a sidekick, kinda like Lawrence Block has in his Scudder series, so I spent two days cataloging expressions."

"Half a million dollars," I said, this time more to myself than to her.

"Yep. That's a lot of cheddar. You want me to add that to your message to Captain Allen?"

"Sure," I said.

I thanked her and hung up. Was it possible the two men had made half a million dollars from bongo night? Sure, the place had been filled with partiers who benefited from a competent bartender, but even if the venue were at maximum capacity and every person racked up a hundred-dollar bar tab, that would be twenty-five thousand dollars. And that was before compensating the band or paying for booze.

Twenty-five thousand dollars was no small change for one night, but half a million?

Half a million dollars seemed a lot more possible if Eric and his friend had done something illegal, and this overheard conversation framed the trouble I'd had with my credit card in a whole new light. I didn't know details or the extent of their crime, but none of that would matter if they figured out I knew. It was one more seemingly unrelated thing that I strongly suspected was related to everything else.

The rest of Sunday passed without hearing from Tex. I grew more anxious by the hour. It was unlike him not to return my call unless he had a solid police-captain reason, so every time I picked up my phone to try again, I set it back down. I swapped out my tunic for another of the high school teacher's pinpoint oxfords, this one lavender (and far less worn than the blue one) and applied the polyurethane sealant on the wood walls in my sitting room.

I threw open the windows to air the place out and took Rocky on a scouting trip through the neighborhood to look for discarded furniture. Sundays had always been profitable in terms of freebies, and today was no different. We netted two aluminum TV stands, a globe lamp, and three different mismatched end tables. I always wondered why people gave away only one.

THE NEXT MORNING, my body set a record for stiffness. The solution was swimming. I clipped on Rocky's leash, pulled a yellow cotton sundress on over my bathing suit, and arrived at the Gaston Swim Club by six fifteen. I set Rocky up in the dog room, carried my towel to the pool deck, and tucked my hair under a swim cap. I was joined by an unlikely companion: Tex.

I was growing accustomed to the wear and tear that took place on him while he was investigating a case. His hair was messy, as if he'd slept on it wet, and his facial hair was about two days into beard growth. Creases by his eyes indicated he hadn't gotten much sleep lately, though I could give him a run for his money in that category. He had on a T-shirt, swim trunks, and rubber flip-flops.

"Hey," he said.

"Hey," I said back. It seemed as though college had reduced our conversational skills to those of a twenty-two-year-old.

"I wasn't sure you'd show."

"I was tempted to skip, but my joints are screaming for a workout."

He eyebrows dropped down low. "You okay?"

"I'll survive."

There were two outstanding factors to swimming at six fifteen in the morning, one of which was the company of regulars. They were octogenarians, plus or minus a decade, who treated their morning swim with the regimented respect they gave their daily fiber intake. They had little interest in eavesdropping on Tex and me, mostly because those who knew me would ask me point-blank in the locker room when we were alone.

This left us on the pool deck with no one around. "Are you going to the college today?" I asked.

He shook his head. "Classes were canceled. You remember that, right?"

I nodded. "I didn't know if you did."

It felt odd, knowing we shared an experience we didn't talk about, yet after Saturday night, it no longer felt like we were at odds. There was a level of trust, an understanding that we would pick up where we left off when this was over, that settled onto my shoulders like a comforting gravity blanket. The most atypical aspect of my life—a relationship with Tex—had become the most reliable. I guessed it was true; when you release your worries and fears, things tend to work out.

"Imogene told me you called. After I checked on the dean, I went to see Lloyd about the autopsy."

"Did he find anything?"

"Nothing we didn't already know. Gallagher had a large dose of antihistamine in his system. Not lethal but more than the directions suggest. We're working on obtaining medical records to see whether it was prescribed for allergies or if it was over the counter. Official cause of death was asphyxiation. All factors point to him being drugged before getting to his car with the expectation that he'd pass out and die from the exhaust fumes."

"What about the door being jimmied?"

He scratched the side of his stubble. "Doesn't factor. Could be random vandalism, could be a prank. Could be somebody had a crisis of conscience."

"Wouldn't it have been easier to just take the rags out of the exhaust pipe?"

"This way Gallagher would have known he was being threatened. If he took the car to a mechanic to fix the door, the whole set-up would have been discovered. Probably fixed.

No harm, no foul, just a professor who knows someone's trying to send him a message."

"Are you any closer to figuring out who the someone is?"

"So far, just a list of persons of interest. Nothing solid."

I pulled my swim cap on and tucked my hair underneath. "I don't know if Eric is on that list, but if not, he should be." I recounted the conversation I'd overheard outside of Kanin's. "I don't think Eric runs a simple event planning organization. His partner said their profits were half a ticket."

"Imogene told me you asked her about that."

"I've been over it a hundred times, and I can't figure out how they made that profit legally. Either they're selling something on the side, or they're skimming from the top."

Tex's blue eyes pierced mine, and even though I had plenty of practice, I broke eye contact. "What aren't you telling me?" he asked.

"There was a problem with my credit card at the club and I threatened to tell the authorities that about the underage drinking and violation of occupancy limits if they didn't give my card back. When I went back yesterday to pay my bill, I heard them say I might be a problem. Eric said he couldn't get rid of me the way he got rid of Gallagher."

If possible, Tex's face clouded more. "What's on your agenda today?" he asked.

"I thought I'd check on Faye. What about you?"

"I'm going to go see the dean. Hopefully my famous hangover remedy will get me in the door, and I can do some unofficial snooping."

"Shouldn't you have offered that yesterday?"

"I tried. He didn't answer the door."

"Is that suspicious?"

"Not after the way he drank Saturday night. I'd be surprised if he got out of bed."

Our conversation was interrupted by a spry older man who climbed out of the pool next to us. "You young people want the lane? I'm all done."

"Sure," I said at the same time Tex said, "No, thanks."

"Better figure out which one it is," the man said. "Got an eager crowd heading this way." He pointed at the locker room, where three eighty-year-old ladies in floral bathing suits had emerged.

Tex stepped back and gestured to the empty lane. "It's all yours."

"Why'd you come if you weren't going to work out?"

He raised one eyebrow and slowly scanned me in my bathing suit. His gaze returned to my face. "Have a good swim, Night." He winked and left.

2 8

I swam long enough to work out the kinks and then added half an hour to clear my mind. By the time I finished, every lane was full. I changed in the locker room, collected Rocky from the puppy room, and left.

Checking on Faye hadn't been a full-blown plan until I said it out loud to Tex. It struck me after the fact that Faye hadn't been with anyone at Kanin's. She left with me and hadn't mentioned saying goodbye to friends. She'd been up and down in class, acting uninterested one moment and asking questions in lecture hall in the other. The same night she'd commented on the value of older men, she stormed out of the class as if she had no intention of returning. It added up to one thing: she was troubled by something.

I parked the truck in a vacant space two blocks from where the golf cart had dropped Faye off and prepped Rocky for whatever we might find. The sun was bright, and the quad was hot. It was a perfect late September day, not too humid, and I wondered how easy it would be, on a day like this when classes were in session, to blow them off and enjoy the weather. A few students entered or exited the library, but for the most part, the campus was quiet.

I pulled a small vest out of my handbag and slipped it around Rocky's torso. The benefit to having been in a number of dangerous situations was that it was easy to have Rocky registered as a service dog. People were often surprised, as I was, to learn there was no formal certification required. Nor was there a training protocol. What I needed was a disability that directly affected my quality of life and a dog to perform tasks to help with said disability. An ACL, torn multiple times, some while fighting off killers, fit the bill. Rocky, having gone for help not unlike Lassie, was a shoe-in. The truth was I didn't require his assistance for much other than emotional support, and the ADA didn't count that. Apparently they'd never met fifty-year-old murder magnets.

We walked to the apartment building and rang the bell. A few minutes later, Faye came to the door. She was dressed in a cropped Van Doren sweatshirt and Batman pajama bottoms. "Madison," Faye said. She seemed surprised to see me. She hunched over and wrapped her arms around her torso. "I don't feel like being around people today." She'd attempted to use makeup to hide dark circles and gaunt cheeks, but the colors were a mismatch to her natural coloring and left her looking like she'd come from a community theater.

"How do you feel today?" I asked. "I don't mean to pry, but you had a rough Saturday night."

"Don't lecture me," she said. It was unclear if she planned to invite me in. It was also unclear if Faye remembered much from Saturday night, including me walking her home.

I'd experienced an unfamiliar form of ageism amongst some of the students, and the feeling returned now. "Take it easy," I said. "We've all had too much to drink at one point or another." I smiled. "You'll feel better by the time classes resume tomorrow."

"I'm not going to classes tomorrow. I'm dropping the whole MBA program."

"You lost your scholarship?"

"Not exactly," she said. I allowed the silence between us to balloon, hoping she'd fill it with an explanation. She did not.

"Faye, you're a bright student, and if you were on a scholarship, then you're obviously qualified for the program. Don't let Professor Gallagher's comment shape your view of business. I don't want to be insensitive, but he's not your professor anymore."

"I'm pregnant," she said suddenly.

She didn't look at me. She kept her head bent down and her eyes fixed on the concrete stoop where I stood. She wrapped her arms around herself, and she hunched her shoulders again. I recognized what I'd mistaken all along: she hadn't had too much to drink last night. She wasn't hung over today. And now, because of an error in judgment, she faced decisions far bigger than how to succeed in business without even trying.

"You're sure?" I asked.

She nodded. "Three positive tests and a confirmation by the health center."

"May I come in?" I asked.

"I'll come out," she said. She joined me on the stoop and pulled the front door behind her. For the first time since I arrived, she seemed to notice Rocky. "Why do you need a service dog?" she asked.

"You know how necessity is the mother of invention?" I asked. She looked at me questioningly. "I'm the girl who invented the necessity for invention."

She laughed. It was the first honest-to-goodness laugh I'd heard from her since I met her, and it took both of us by surprise. "You're nothing like I expected," she said. "That first day when you came into class, I thought you were the teaching aid. I was jealous because you were going to spend a lot of time with Professor Gallagher."

"Eric thought that too. I guess you don't get a lot of people my age in class."

"That's for sure," she said. I smiled at her ignorant insensitivity. We walked side by side across the street and onto the quad. Despite Rocky tugging on the leash, I sensed Faye wanted to rest. "Let's sit," I suggested.

She lowered herself onto a wrought iron bench. "Why did you enroll in school?" she asked.

I sat down and tipped my head back to feel the sun on my face. I closed my eyes and thought back to the day I'd been rejected by every bank in town. It was a little over a week ago, but it felt like months. One small step forward, just acknowledging that maybe I didn't know everything I needed to know, had led me through the gates of Van Doren, and that led me to Gallagher's class. Everything had unfolded in a way I never could have imagined and all because I let go of the notion that I knew what I was doing.

I opened my eyes and stared straight ahead. "Remember the question you asked in lecture hall on Friday? About following your instincts and making a decision that's unpopular with your team?"

She nodded.

"I didn't have a team. It was just me. And I made a mistake that cost me my company. I made the mistake myself, and I thought I could fix it myself. I soon found out the financial world did not share my opinion of my business acumen."

"You should put that in your eight-hundred-word essay," she said.

I smiled and then pointed across the street to the Dallas First National Bank. "See that building?"

"The bank?"

"Yep. They were the last ones to reject my loan application." I pointed at the entrance to the college campus. "See those gates?"

"Yes."

"That was what I saw when I left the bank. After a day of rejection, I felt like I didn't know anything about business, so I came to the one place where I could learn."

Faye leaned back against the bench and kicked her feet out in front of her. "I applied to school here because my friends all applied to school here. My scholarship isn't for academics. It's for volleyball. Pretty soon, I'm not going to be able to play, and I'm going to lose the money anyway." She shrugged.

"You're already here. Don't give up on your opportunity to learn."

"Maybe I'm not cut out for business school," she said.

Her words had a ring of familiarity about them. I'd said the same thing to Eric at the club.

Faye continued. "You have this drive that I don't. Everybody in that class does. I would have died if a professor put me on the spot the way Professor Gallagher did to you."

"You said you were jealous of me when you thought I was the teaching aide because I'd be spending time with him. Wouldn't you like if he singled you out?"

"Not like that. He does that to students to test them. To see how committed they are to the subject matter."

"Did he ever do it to you?"

"No." She stuck her feet out in front of her and tapped the

toes of her sandals together. Her toenails were painted pale pink, and her feet were tan. A shiny silver toe ring decorated the second toe on her left foot. "He didn't see the same thing in me he saw in you."

"You don't know that."

"I do. When Dean Wallace told me to drop the class or I'd fail it, he said Professor Gallagher suggested it in his notes."

"Do you know why?"

She shook her head.

My phone buzzed. I pulled it out. The name Rex was on the screen. When had Tex reprogrammed my phone?

"He likes you," Faye said, not hiding that she'd looked at my screen.

"Who?"

"Rexford Allen. The new guy from class."

"What makes you say that?"

"I saw the way he watched you at Kanin's. You thought— everybody thought—I was drunk, but I wasn't. I just wanted to go out like a normal college student. But I felt nauseous, and, well, you found me in the bathroom. You know I got sick."

"I thought morning sickness happened in the morning."

"You've never been pregnant?"

"No," I said. "Motherhood wasn't in the cards for me."

She misunderstood my answer and gave me a sad smile. We sat next to each other while the sun cast fading rays across the grass. Despite our contrast in ages, we'd tiptoed up to the brink of girl talk, so I took the liberty of jumping off the cliff. "Does the father know?" I asked softly.

She shrugged.

"Faye, you need to tell him. He has a right to know."

"I can't talk to him. Not anymore."

Considering how close they had to have been to make this happen, the follow-up conversation should have been easy. "You feel alone right now. Like you can't talk to anybody. You just told me, and that wasn't so hard, was it?" She shook her head but didn't look my way. "You don't have to be alone if you don't want. It's your choice."

"You don't understand. I can't talk to him. He's—"

"He's what? Whatever you think, you're probably imagining the worst."

"He's dead. The father was Professor Gallagher."

2 9

"You... and Professor Gallagher?" I asked. It seemed almost unbelievable.

She looked at me with fearful eyes. "You won't say anything, will you? Not to anybody?"

It was a promise I couldn't keep. "Faye, you need to talk to someone. Not just because of your circumstances but because of what happened to the professor. It's a lot to process."

"The last time I talked to someone about this, something bad happened."

It no longer felt like we were having a casual conversation between students. Tex had said something—what was it?—that Gallagher had accusations of sexual harassment from students at the last school he worked for. Even if Faye was of age, this information would have been potentially damaging to his career. I immediately understood why he would want it to stay quiet, but I also wondered what someone might do if they knew.

"Faye, who did you talk to?" I asked.

"Barbara. At the admissions desk. She caught me going

into William's office from the back door and confronted me, and I broke down."

It took me a moment to realize the William in her story was Professor Gallagher, though based on what she'd just confessed, it made sense that they might have been on first-name basis. "What happened?"

"I told her I thought he and I had a relationship, but then he just turned his back on me, and I didn't understand what I did wrong."

A faint memory returned, the sound of a door slamming inside Gallagher's office the day I went to get his permission to join his class. Nothing had seemed out of the ordinary at the time, but someone could have accessed his office and confronted him, or even just brought him a cup of coffee that was heavily laced with an antihistamine.

Barbara knew Gallagher's schedule and had even made mention of the blonde who met with him after class. At the time, I'd written her response off, but she clearly had an opinion about the professor and his extracurricular activities. How many times had she seen something like this? How easy would it have been to keep looking the other way?

"What did she say?" I asked. I took extra care to modulate my voice.

"She said not to worry about my classes or my scholarship and to take care of myself. She was nice about the whole thing, nicer than I expected. She's usually so stern, but she said she'd talk to the professor for me. And then—"

And then he'd been killed.

I had questions. Lots more questions. But Faye wasn't the person I needed to ask. As if she recognized the shift in my energy, she dropped her feet to the ground and stood up. "I have to go."

I put my hand on her arm. "Faye wait." She didn't leave but didn't make eye contact. "Will there be a memorial for the professor tomorrow?"

She shook her head. "I asked around, but nobody cared enough to plan one." She swiped a tear from her eye and then stepped away. "I have to go."

I tried to follow her, but Rocky had wound his leash around the bench, and after two steps in Faye's direction, the tension on the leash pulled me back. Faye hurried across the quad toward the campus housing.

Faye and Professor Gallagher?

Faye and Professor Gallagher.

Was that why he made notes in his file that she wasn't suited for the class? A crisis of conscience, or was this a pattern with him? Was that the risk *he* took for reward? And what exactly had transpired during that conversation with Barbara? Had she accused him, or threatened to turn him in, or did she have it in her to do something worse? I couldn't see her sabotaging the professor's car, but I didn't discount the possibility that she could hire someone else to do so. A mother hen, surrounded by roosters, might be moved to take extreme measures to protect her chicks.

I returned Tex's call. After answering, he said, "We're done with your car, but you need to take it to a body shop."

"I talked to Mickey this morning."

"Did you take the Mustang?"

"I took the truck."

"Mickey owes me fifty bucks."

It always surprised me how the police were able to maintain their interest in bets while conducting a murder investigation. "I'm at the college, and I—"

"Not now, Night. Thanks." He hung up.

I understood the delicate nature of dating the captain of the police. By proximity, I was privy to information the general public would not know. And depending on who was in the office with him, he had to be careful about what he shared with me. But this information from Faye related to his case, and I had to make sure he knew about it.

I called the front desk. "Lakewood Police Department," Imogene answered.

"This is Madison. Is Captain Allen available?"

"He was just going to call you about your car. He's in his office with the police commissioner. Do you want me to interrupt them?"

That explained Tex not being able to talk. "No, that's not necessary. Can you give him a message? Let him know I have new information regarding the murder of Professor William Gallagher."

She dropped her voice. "Can you tell me?"

"I think it's best if the information goes directly to Captain Allen. Let's let him decide what he's willing to share. Is there a tip line for the case?" For the first time since Professor Gallagher died, I realized how far removed I'd been from the news. "If there is, I must have missed it."

"There is, and guess what? It's me. I mean, it's a machine, but I screen the messages as they come in and give the captain updates as needed. I guess you can tell me after all."

I'd feel a whole lot better about this if I'd heard it from Tex, but it was clear he wasn't available. "Tell him Faye Talbot is pregnant and Professor Gallagher is the father."

"Faye—pregnant—Gallagher—father. Got it. Is he hot?"

"Who?"

"The professor. College girls always want to sleep with the hot professors."

"You do know Gallagher is the murder victim, right?"

"Doesn't mean he can't be hot. It adds more to the plot. Were his colleagues jealous? Was this a pattern for him? Did any of the parents know? Was he married? Is the college afraid of a lawsuit? If he was a dud, then some of that drops away. Hold on."

The phone went silent, and I sat impatiently, wondering if Tex and the commissioner had finished their business. The phone clicked again, and Imogene returned. "Sorry about that. You gave me an idea for a plot twist."

"Have Captain Allen call me when he's done," I said. "And good luck with your book."

***

I DIDN'T HEAR from Tex for the rest of the day. It wasn't for lack of trying. After leaving messages on each of his phones, I went home. The fumes from Saturday's work were gone, and the knotty pine walls were dry. I stood in the center of the room and turned in a circle, imagining the rest of it. I stopped when I reached the front window. I'd been looking for an opportunity to order from Beauti-Vue's Retro old stock of woven wood, and this room would be perfect.

I clicked through the swatches on their website and chose "Planet," a rust, blue, and cream shade that fit the astronaut portion of the design concept, at least in name. I measured the window and placed my order, complete with blue pom-pom trim. Already I could see a low-back sofa along the far wall, something tweed with wooden cone legs. I'd have to be thoughtful when it came to hanging art; anything too kitschy would turn the design from classic to parody in a snap.

I was all out of Lean Cuisines, so I microwaved one of

Tex's Hungry Man Smokin' Backyard Barbeque meals. (Rocky got one too.) Texans all over the place were rolling their eyes.

I called the credit card company and canceled my card to be on the safe side and then took Rocky out for his last walk of the day. I'd like to say I had a productive evening at home, but the reality was less interesting: I changed into a pale pink peignoir set and crawled into bed. It was far more comfortable than sleeping on the floor of the property next door, and I'm not ashamed to say I was asleep by nine.

***

Tex was waiting for me in the kitchen the next morning. His Shih-Chi puppy, Wojo, was curled up on Rocky's dog bed, and Rocky sat outside of it with his furry head propped on the side. The two had become fast friends and enjoyed playdates while Tex and I enjoyed playdates of a different nature. I hadn't expected Tex to come over, and I wore little more than my pink peignoir set. His pupils dilated when he saw me. He set his coffee cup down and pulled me toward him.

"You look great," he said.

"You look like shit."

He nuzzled my neck. "I always look like shit. Gives me street cred."

I laughed and put my hands on his chest. "Do you still need street cred if you're the captain?"

"We're all doing double duty. Until we get an approved budget, I'm as valuable on the street as my team."

It was a subtle shift, Tex referring to his unit as a team and not as his men. I'd watched these changes happen, little by little, over the years I'd known him.

"I didn't expect to see you until graduation," I said. "What with me dropping out and all."

"About that. You sure that's what you want to do?"

"I don't know what I want to do. I just know I want to do something. This"—I waved my hands around in circles—"all feels temporary."

"Your house feels temporary?"

"No, the house is the one thing that doesn't feel temporary."

"Do we feel temporary?"

"No, we feel, well, we feel less temporary than we used to."

"What about Mad for Mod?"

"That." I pointed at him. "That's what feels temporary. The empty showroom. The lack of clients. I feel like I should be *doing* something about that, not sitting around talking about it."

Tex went to the stove. Spread out across the countertop was a pink and white CorningWare mixing bowl, my vintage pink hand blender, a carton of eggs, butter, sugar, and a loaf of bread. "Have a seat," he said. "I'll make you French toast."

"You're making me breakfast?"

"I took out your trash. I can't risk people finding out my girlfriend eats Hungry Man Barbecue."

"Rocky ate one too."

"That doesn't make it better."

I grabbed a mug from the cabinet and filled it with hot coffee then hovered by Tex's elbow. He turned. "Sit. Relax. Drink your coffee. There's creamer on the table."

"I drink it black like you."

"Yes, but I make it stronger than you like." He nodded at the table. "Sit. Relax. Drink your coffee," he repeated.

I wasn't used to having Tex make me breakfast. Truthfully,

I wasn't used to anyone making me breakfast, me included. It was a welcome treat.

"I don't want to ruin the mood, but I have some information that relates to your case."

"Sit. Relax. Drink you—"

"Is that why you're making me breakfast?" I asked. "Distraction?"

He held the pan over a Franciscan Swingtime dinnerplate, one of an incomplete collection I'd acquired from the estate of a local golf champion. The pattern was introduced in 1959, the same year *Pillow Talk* released, which might have been the reason it was my favorite. The plates were white with gentle lines and airy pink and green geometric shapes that suggested movement and direction. Two pieces of French toast slipped out of the pan on top of the pattern on the plate. Tex reached into a bag of sugar and then held his hand over the top and let the granules trickle down onto the bread. He tossed a dish towel over his shoulder and set the plate in front of me. "Eat."

"Oooh, a new word. Was there a vocabulary lesson in Cavemen 101?"

He grinned and then sat catacorner to me.

"Did you get any of my messages yesterday? I left one with Imogene."

"It's not relevant," he said.

"How can you dismiss it so quickly? You don't think it's curious a professor got a student pregnant? Especially now, after the professor was murdered?"

Tex waited a few seconds after I finished, and the word "murdered" hung in the air. I was tempted to say something else to end on a more pleasant note, but he spoke. "I can tell you things that relate to you finding the body, and I can caution you away from things that would put you in danger. But I can't talk to you about the case."

We'd been here before.

The one-sided nature of our conversations regarding Tex's cases was frustrating, and while I understood it, I didn't like it.

He seemed to understand my vexation. "When we were classmates," he said, "I could ask questions around you that may have, with the knowledge you already had, led you to draw certain conclusions. And when we ended up at the same nightclub and our professor needed help getting home, you may have picked up information not available to the public. It was unavoidable."

"Yes, I can see how all of that might have happened."

I sliced into my French toast and raised a bite to my mouth. He'd added a touch of Himalayan sea salt and some local honey, both ingredients I wouldn't have expected, and the resulting flavors were magnified. The texture of the salt on the surface of my tongue contrasted with the smooth honey and chewy bread. I took another bite.

I swallowed and pointed at my plate. "Yum." I added, "can we not talk for a moment? I want to sit, relax, drink coffee, and eat."

"By all means, continue." He pulled his coffee mug toward him and took a long swig and then leaned back. He looked up at the ceiling and then turned his head and looked through the living room toward the sitting room. "You need me to do anything around here? Replace lightbulbs or change your AC filters?"

"That's it." I set my knife and fork down. "What do you want?"

"Me? I'm just offering to help you out."

"You made me breakfast. You put cream on the table. You

let Rocky out so I could sleep late. And you're offering to do small tasks around the house. I know you too well to think otherwise. What do you want, Captain Allen?"

He reached forward and snatched a piece of toast off my plate. "Captain Allen doesn't need a favor from you."

"What do you want, Tex?"

"Tex doesn't want a favor from you either." He bit into a piece of toast and washed it down with a slug of coffee. "Rexford Allen needs a favor from you."

This was worse than *The Three Faces of Eve*!

"The other night in class, when Ling came to talk to you, Hugo put me on the hot seat. He told me to share my business plan with the class."

"Where did you get a business plan?"

He reached over to the counter and picked up a shiny red folder. He set it in front of me and tapped the cover. "Here," he said.

"That's my business prospectus. That was what I took to the banks."

"I know. I passed it off as mine to protect my cover."

"I'm surprised he didn't fail you on the spot."

"He was impressed. More than impressed, I'd say. He pulled me aside after class and said there was nothing an MBA was going to give me that I didn't already know."

"Do you think he suspects something? Was he trying to get you to drop the class?"

"That's one way of looking at it," he said. "The other way is that this"—he tapped my folder again—"is a solid business plan, and he knows it. I took out everything that related back to you. The dean of business for Van Doren College was so impressed he suggested the class go off-campus to check out my store tomorrow night. I told him I haven't officially opened, so the place was still being set up, but he insisted."

"I see," I said, because the special breakfast, the use of my favorite plates, the playdate for Rocky, and the whole picture became increasingly clear. "You need me to design you a hat store."

Tex grinned, and I knew I'd hit the nail on the head. "I contacted Bill's Western Warehouse and arranged to borrow from their backstock to get inventory. I'm not sure what it'll take to make it work, but I was hoping you could handle details."

"You're such a thoughtful guy," I said.

"If you need help, call Virginia."

"The stripper?"

"Night, I can't have you calling in your cavalry on this one. The less people who know the truth, the better. Virginia helped me out once, and she knows how to keep her mouth shut."

I rolled my eyes in a classic Doris Day expression. "Any other suggestions?" I asked. "Maybe the girl you took to your high school prom is available."

"Call Imogene," he added. "She's a civilian volunteer, but she knows the case."

"You're not worried this will turn up in her book?"

"If it does, I'll make sure you look good." He turned on the boyish charm. "I'll make the calls. Might be better coming from me. Normally I wouldn't take a cover story this far, but with what we know about the dean, I want to keep him in my sights."

I agreed to cut classes and help Tex for a price to be named later. He agreed to take the dogs for the day, so after breakfast, I went upstairs and got ready. I returned half an hour later, freshly scrubbed and dressed in powder blue knit stirrup pants and a boxy short-sleeved pullover in coordinating panels of blue and brown. It was remarkable how many women owned colorful stirrup pants in the sixties; I could wear a pair a day for a year and not repeat once.

"Don't forget about that pink number you were wearing earlier. I'd like it to stay in rotation."

I pointed at the stove. "Don't forget that making-me-breakfast routine either."

He pretended to take a punch to the chest. "Tough negotiator."

"I'm in business school," I said, "I might just be the teacher's pet."

We kissed, and I left. Now that we'd worked past the tension that came with the case, there was a level of freedom in our relationship that existed behind the walls of our respective living spaces. Questions, rumors, and gossip didn't exist. We no longer actively tried to hide that we were involved, but the situation at the college had made it so anyway. At least we were in practice.

I parked behind my storefront and let myself in through the back door. There was a short hallway that led to my former office on the right and a small powder room on the left. Past both was the main showroom. The street-facing view was floor-to-ceiling windows, which allowed me to maintain rotating displays to attract clients. Behind them I'd grouped seating, and in the back, on a raised platform my former handyman Hudson James had installed for me, I kept an assortment of tables, chairs, and lamps. Everything I showcased was available through a design job, and on occasion, someone fell in love with a piece and I worked around it. A constant source of inspiration were the light fixtures inspired by Sputnik.

But today wasn't about space-age lighting or Danish Modern furniture or Tiki bars. It was about western wear. It was ironic; to get back on the horse of Mad for Mod, I was going to be dealing in cowboy hats.

I put the soundtrack for *Calamity Jane* on my portable CD player and started cleaning the place. Even empty showrooms collected dust, and in the months of inactivity, it settled in all the wrong places. I vacuumed, dusted, washed the windows, and even used a razor to scrape off my now-faded logo. I designed and ordered a new window decal from a local sign shop and paid extra for same-day pickup.

A truck from Bill's Western Warehouse parked out front. The driver was a burly man in a white straw cowboy hat and plaid shirt over a white T-shirt. I unlocked the door and greeted him through the truck widow.

"There's a lot out back for unloading," I said.

He waved me off. "Not necessary. I got a couple of cartons, and this'll be easier than navigating around the corner."

I stood back and looked at the length of the truck. "A couple of cartons? I thought we were borrowing enough inventory to fill the store." I pointed over my shoulder. Can't you call the owner?

"I am the owner. I'm Bill, of Bill's Western Warehouse. I've got a convention coming through this week. I packed up the clearance and a couple of slow movers, but that's the best I can do."

"How many are we talking about?"

"Couple dozen."

I turned around and looked inside the store. I could fit a couple dozen hats in the front window alone. "Did you talk to Captain Allen?"

"He told me to talk to you, so I'm talking to you." He pointed at the door. "You want me to drop them off inside?"

"Sure." I turned around and wedged a stopper under the front door. This plan was going to go bust before it even got full-blown.

Bill opened the back of his truck and pulled out a dolly then stacked two D-containers on top and wheeled them in.

"Nice space," he said. "The police must have called in a favor from a vacant storefront too. Good location."

"Yes, it is," I said, not commenting on the police favor aspect of his commentary.

He tapped the top of the carton. "You plan to fill this place?"

"I was hoping to."

"Time to get creative."

While we spoke, a convertible BMW pulled up behind his truck. Virginia got out. She wore a tight, low-cut red sweater and cuffed jean shorts with ankle socks and white leather sneakers. Her blond hair was pulled into ponytails, and her lipstick matched her shirt. She came into the store and greeted me. Bill took one look at her, and his eyes went wide. "Virginia? What are you doin' here?"

"I'm helpin' out Captain Allen just like you," she said with a wink.

He smiled at her and then turned back to me. "And how do you two know each other?"

"We're—" I started.

"—colleagues," Virginia finished.

Bill looked back and forth between us, and his smile widened. "Well, I'll be." He opened a carton and pulled out a white felt hat and placed it on Virginia's head. "You ladies wait right here. I might be able to help you out with a few more hats."

I directed Virginia to park her car in the back while Bill scrounged up three additional cartons of inventory. It still wasn't enough, but it was something.

Imogene arrived while Virginia was trying to flirt another case of hats out of Bill. (It was possible the flirtation was in my imagination; for all I knew, they were talking sports.)

Imogene was an attractive strawberry blonde in her mid-forties. She had bright blue eyes and a spattering of freckles across her nose, and I imagined this was what Trixie Belden might look like if she were an adult. Imogene was dressed in a checkered shirt, slim capri pants, and ballet flats. She wore a black nylon messenger bag across her torso. "Before we get started, can I go over something with you?" she asked.

"Me? Sure."

She pulled a notebook and pen out of her bag and prepared to take notes. "When you called yesterday, you said the victim got a girl pregnant, right?" She flipped a page forward. "'Suspect—pregnant—victim—father.' Right?"

"Suspect? Victim? Does this have to do with Captain Allen's case?"

"Of course not. I mean, I don't know enough to talk about except what I see on the news and what I pick up around the coffee maker, but I can't talk to anybody about it."

"Then what's this about?" I asked. I pointed at her notebook.

"Plot twist. I make notes, but I don't use names. It sounds like it means something, right? If there was a jealous husband or the suspect was underage, maybe somebody would want to kill him, but Captain Allen said the facts didn't line up. I figure it's fair game for a book."

"How is that possible?" I said, more to myself than to her. "He got a student pregnant. How is that not relevant?"

"He didn't say it wasn't relevant. He said the facts didn't line up, and he's right. They don't."

"I don't understand."

"Simple. The professor couldn't get anybody pregnant. According to the autopsy, he had a vasectomy."

"Are you sure?" I asked Imogene. This new information flew in the face of Faye's facts.

"Sure, I'm sure," she said. She ran her fingers though her wavy blond bob. "I checked the file myself."

This distracted me from the initial question. "Does Captain Allen know you checked the file?"

She shrugged. "I have a certain amount of autonomy at the front desk."

I let that one go and circled back to the important piece of information: if Gallagher hadn't gotten Faye pregnant, then who had?

Behind Imogene, Virginia bade goodbye to Bill and joined us. "Who's pregnant?" she asked. She looked at both of our bellies. "Are we talking reality TV?"

I pointed to Imogene and made introductions. "This is Imogene. She's a mystery writer. She's working out a plot point. Imogene, this is Virginia. She's... a freelancer."

"You're the dancer!" Imogene exclaimed. "Captain Allen

told me about you. You'd make a great character. Do you mind if I pick your brain?"

This could go very wrong very quickly. Before things got out of hand, I spelled out the plan.

"Ladies, we have eight hours to turn this place into a hat store. I have to pick up a sign from the printer and find us some fixtures. Can you two work on unpacking the inventory? There should be packing lists in the cartons."

"Darlin', I don't want to be a buzzkill, but shouldn't a hat store have more than seven cartons of hats?" Virginia asked. (She'd scored us two more.)

"We could use mirrors," Imogene said. "Don't decorators always suggest mirrors to make a room look bigger?"

"Not always," I answered. "But we do need mirrors, for the customers. Good call." I made a quick note while Imogene looked pleased with herself. "We can screen off the back half of the showroom. Nobody has to know how big the store is."

It was a lame solution to a legitimate concern. Tex was going to lose all credibility with the dean if I didn't come up with something better.

And I realized I did have something better. I had a whole collection of something better—the boxes of men's clothing from the building once owned by Sam Johnson, along with whatever I might find in the boxes in my attic.

I left Imogene and Virginia to sort through the hats and drove to the sign shop. It felt good to have a purpose. Even if western wear wasn't my passion project, I had something to focus on that lit me up. But Virginia's question nagged at me. Tex had wowed the dean with his (my) business prospectus, but if the store didn't fit the picture, Hugo would get suspicious. And if he was a suspect, the last thing we wanted was for him see to through us.

The window decal was near-perfect: Rexford Allen Stetsons, curved over an outline of a cowboy hat. I asked them to add the words And More across the bottom. They were too busy, they said, but directed me to a rack of clearance decals with typos. Aunt Betty's Polish Peirogis and More—that fit the bill. Problem solved for the low price of a 50% off decal and a pair of scissors.

I called Joanie. "I got a new car," I said.

"Since the truck? I saw Mickey last night, and he didn't say that. Or do you mean your Alfa? You didn't trade in your Alfa Romeo, did you?"

"Not my *car* car. My business. Remember how you said Mad for Mod was a broken-down junker?"

"Don't put words in my mouth."

"You said—"

"I know what I said."

"I figured out how to move forward." I told her about Rexford Allen's Stetsons and More.

"You're opening a men's clothing store?" she asked.

"No, Tex, or should I say, *Rex* is opening a men's clothing store. A pop-up shop. Not so much opening as expanding from cowboy hats to vintage western and formal wear. Did you know Thelma Johnson's husband ran a clothing store?"

"Stay in your lane, Madison. I appreciate that you liked my metaphor, but you're all over the road right now."

"I recently discovered I'm the proud owner of a whole bunch of western wear thanks to Sam Johnson—Thelma's husband—and a hurricane in the eighties. And I have an attic filled with vintage men's clothing from all of the estates I've bought out."

"I thought you sold men's clothes off by the carton."

"I've bought out a *lot* of estates. I didn't even realize how much stuff I had."

The benefit of sharing my idea with Joanie was that she caught on quickly. "A pop-up shop that nobody knows is a pop-up shop. Genius. You set up a fake store to help Tex with his cover and host a blow-out sale. You're using your studio, right? Good Feng Shui. Clear the stagnant energy by the front door. You can invest the profits into Mad for Mod and reopen before you know it."

"It'll work, right?"

"It has all the earmarks of a very good idea."

I went home and climbed into the attic. The air smelled like wood and dust. In the ceiling, a small turbine spun erratically, pulling in morning air and stirring up particles that floated through beams of sunlight. I pulled the chain on the overhead bulb to illuminate the attic further and went to the back where I kept cartons of clothes I'd never considered wearing for one reason: they were for men.

Most of the estates I purchased were left behind by women who had outlived their husbands, and in many cases, they'd simply boxed up their husband's belongings and shoved them into an attic themselves. I'd sold a few off here and there, but when my business took off, the efforts of dealing with clothing sales took up time better used elsewhere. This was a classic case of out of sight, out of mind; I'd all but forgotten I had this stuff. But having seen the clothes left behind by Sam Johnson next door and being in need of capital quickly, I noticed that separate thoughts had coalesced into an idea. I wouldn't make enough for a loan, but I'd make enough for a deposit. And enough to show the banks that how I looked on paper didn't matter as much as the paper I deposited into my account.

I transferred several cartons of clothes from the attic to the back of the truck and returned to Mad for Mod—I mean, Rexford Allen's Stetsons and More, parked the truck out back, and went inside. The place smelled like Febreze, a significant improvement over musty, stale air. Virginia was teaching Imogene a dance move that had nothing to do with mystery writing. I raised my eyebrows at them and then shook off the visual.

"Ladies," I said. "New plan." I held up the window decal. "We're now an 'And More.'" I held up the sign.

"Someone suggested 'and more' at Jumbo's and got fired," Virginia said. "I guess that's a whole different business model."

"The world's oldest," Imogene quipped.

I went to my office to make a phone call. Having a project on which to focus took my mind off the homicide, which might have been Tex's goal. But it also reminded me of what I'd learned after a week of business school: it took big risks to get big rewards. I hoped the lesson was sound because I was about to risk everything on a full-blown, get-my-life-back plan that hinged on step number one, and step number one was a doozy.

I called Nasty.

"Big Bro," she answered.

"Donna, it's Madison." I chose my opening sentence carefully and spoke her language. "I have a business proposition for you." I gave her a moment to roll her eyes/ reply/ hang up.

"Where are you?"

"Mad for Mod."

"Meet me at Benny's Bagels. I'll be there in ten minutes."

I beat Nasty by two minutes. She arrived with Huxley strapped against her chest with a convertible ergonomic baby carrier. He wore a green onesie and matching knit cap. Under the baby carrier, Nasty wore a navy blue yoga ensemble, white ankle socks and New Balance sneakers. Her hair was pulled back in a ponytail, and she carried a diaper bag that matched Huxley's harness.

Rocky had exhausted all the smells that came from the base of the table and shifted his attention to Nasty's sneakers. She set her bag in the chair opposite me.

"I'll be right back," she said and then went inside. Rocky returned to my side and looked up at me as if questioning my motivation.

"Act cool, Rock," I said to him. "I have a plan."

He paced back and forth a few times and then sat down next to my chair.

Nasty returned with a green juice and sat, keeping one hand gently rubbing back and forth on Huxley's back. "You got my attention with that phone call," she said. "Plus you caught me right after yoga. Good move."

"You take your baby to yoga?"

"Mommy and Me Yoga. I don't love the name, but it's a meditative experience. You should try yoga. You might like it."

"I prefer swimming."

"Right," she said. "So, tell me about this business opportunity." She took a sip of her green juice.

This was it. Step one. Off a cliff.

"I'd like you to buy me out of the apartment building on Gaston Avenue," I said. "You invested in the renovation and made your money back in the first two months. You know the property is a good investment."

She leaned back. "If I'm not mistaken, that building is your sole source of income."

"You'll pay me an annual salary to oversee the property.

I've been doing it since, well, since I lost my business. I know the tenants. I know what's involved."

"You aren't going to give up your decorating business to become a property manager," she said, more a statement of fact than a question.

"With the money from the sale, I want to buy the building next to my house. It's zoned for commercial use. It will become a satellite showroom for Mad for Mod. I'll keep the original location on Greenville Avenue and open a second location by my house and hire someone to manage one while I manage the other. I'll double my business in a year."

"And what happens when one of the tenants in the apartment building needs a new lightbulb? You only manage the place now because you have the time."

"I can do both. Mad for Mod conceived, designed, and renovated the entire property. It's part of my portfolio. I already know how to fix anything that needs fixing and who to call if I can't do it myself. You'll—as the apartment building owner—be on my books as a client. Decorating gives me a certain amount of autonomy, which will provide the flexibility to handle issues as they arise or hire out someone to handle them for me."

She reached behind her head and pulled her ponytail around to the front. Huxley's little fist reached out and grabbed it. Nasty didn't seem to mind. As I sat across from her, I wondered about how fast her life moved and how little downtime she had.

"No," she said after a moment of thought. "It won't work. Your passion is your decorating business, not property management."

My hope deflated. "Donna, this is a means to an end. When I reopen Mad for Mod, I want to expand. The property next to my house makes sense. I could use the land behind it as a display for outdoor decorating, which is a new market for me. I can show twice as many examples of what I can do, and since that building is commercially zoned, I can sell merchandise or rent it out for classes. You remember Mitchell from Paintin' Place, right?" She nodded. "He's involved with a local design school. There's no reason I can't get him to work with me."

She pointed at me. "That's passion. *That's* what I want to invest in."

"That's what I'm asking you to do."

"No, Madison. You're overcomplicating things. You don't want to manage an apartment building. You want money. It's okay to say it."

"Money solves a number of my problems, yes."

She patted Huxley's back. He pulled her ponytail to his mouth and chewed on it. She took to motherhood like she took to everything else. Like it was the most natural thing in the world. She'd even made pregnancy hormones work for her.

"How's business school?" she asked.

I was happy to have a shift in conversation. "It's good," I said automatically. But was it good? Was I even still enrolled? "I don't know whether it's good or not. The dean moved Radical Business Strategy to a night class after Professor Gallagher was murdered and took over the curriculum, but I already had a full day of classes so by the time it starts, I'm wiped out. The dean said something about giving me course credit for my business experience, but maybe business school isn't right for me."

"You already know everything you need to know," she said. "You've lived the syllabus. You don't need a degree."

"Yes, but I don't know how to show the banks that."

She leaned back. "Here's my offer. We'll go to the bank together. You spell out your plan. I'll co-sign the paperwork. If you fail to make payments, your business defaults to me. The moment you pay off your loans, I'm out. Deal?"

"I don't want a partner," I said.

"Don't focus on what you don't want. Tell me what you do. What do you want, Madison?"

"I want to reopen my business and expand."

"And what will it take to make that happen?"

"Money."

She studied me. "How much do you need?"

I'd crunched the numbers and knew the answer. "A hundred thousand dollars gets me a down payment, a cushion on rent for the Greenville Avenue location, and enough to buy a couple estates for inventory."

"What about systems, staff, advertising? Dream bigger, Madison. How sure are you that your expansion plan will pay off?"

"One hundred percent."

"Nobody's one hundred percent. Look what happened to you. You were unprepared because you thought your business was bulletproof. Allow room for disaster."

"Ninety-nine and forty-four one hundredths."

She allowed a tiny sliver of a smile. "You and Ivory soap. Figures." She finished her juice and set the empty plastic cup on the center of the table. "Do you trust me?"

Maybe.

I'd thought many things of Nasty over the years, not all of them complimentary. I knew she wouldn't do this if she didn't know it would be good for her too. Maybe that was what did it. Maybe it was because by offering, she cast a confidence-building vote in my direction, and maybe confidence in my business decisions was the one thing I needed more than money.

"Yes," I said.

She held out her hand, and I shook it. And then Huxley threw up on her shoulder, demonstrating exactly how I felt.

Nasty excused herself and went to the restroom to clean up. I bussed our table. When she returned, I stood and unwound Rocky's leash.

"When do you want to do this?" I asked. "I'll make an appointment with the loan officer whenever you're free."

"Let's go now."

I didn't plan to look at her yoga attire, but I felt myself assess her outfit in the same way a sales associate at an upscale store judged a potential customer by the condition of their shoes. "Don't you want to change?"

"Banks don't care what you wear," she said. "They care if you can repay their money on a schedule."

"My paperwork is at home," I said.

"Don't sweat it. You have everything you need between your ears." She put on a pair of Tom Ford sunglasses. "I didn't see your car. Where'd you park?"

I pointed at the pick-up truck. "My car is at police impound. I'm driving that."

"Nice work, Madison. Now I know what we're going to talk about on the way."

———

DESPITE NASTY'S offer to drive, I followed her in the truck. I didn't know how much about the vandalism would be public knowledge, and while Nasty wasn't exactly the public, she was a businesswoman who specialized in security and might use the information for professional gain. That alone kept me from telling her everything.

General traffic and my unfamiliarity with driving a pick-up truck allowed her to arrive before me. I parked the truck next to her silver Saab, pulled a brush out of my handbag and combed Rocky's fur, gave myself a pep talk, and then got out. The campus across the street was bustling with student energy, a stark contrast to yesterday's peaceful quiet.

I entered the bank and let Rocky lead the way. I always marveled at how easily he detected a path, based not on purpose but by curiosity. He sniffed a few tables here and there but ultimately drew me toward Nasty, who was already seated in front of Pete Cross, the loan officer who had turned me down. Huxley was resting in a portable crib on the chair next to her. Rocky stuck his nose in the air and sniffed and then trotted over toward the two of them, leaving me no choice but to follow.

"Madison," Pete said. Today he wore a green suit, white shirt, and cranberry necktie with piano keys. "Have a seat. Donna was just filling me in on your circumstances."

There were two seats, and they were occupied by mother and baby. Neither made a move to move. Pete got up. "I'll get you a chair." He quickly returned with a third seat that he put alongside Huxley. I sat, Rocky sniffed, and Huxley waved his fists.

"You know my circumstances," I said to Pete. "You rejected my application just last week." I didn't expect to say that. Perhaps Nasty should have coached me in the parking lot?

Pete acted as though I hadn't said anything. "Donna said you found a second location that was perfect for your business expansion."

I looked from him to Nasty. She gave me an almost imperceptible shrug. I turned back to Pete. "Yes. It was originally built by the owners of my house but sold off when the husband died."

"Tell me about your plans for the property."

I'd told enough people that by now, the concept flowed out of me as if I were taking an oral exam. I talked about the building proximity to my house, the possibility of expanding into outdoor decorating, the commercial zoning that allowed for retail transactions or classroom rental space. I ended with a ballpark timetable of how long it would take for me to get up and running if a loan were approved and a corresponding ballpark for how quickly I could pay the loan back. There were so many ballparks in my response that I expected a stadium vendor to show up and sell us peanuts.

Pete turned to Nasty. "You're right. She knows her stuff."

"She's a good risk," Nasty said. "Aside from one error in judgment, I've never seen her make a mistake when it comes to her business."

"Okay, then. Let me draw up the paperwork, and we'll be all set. Donna suggested two fifty. Is that enough to get you started?"

"Two fifty?"

"Two hundred and fifty thousand dollars at six percent.

That's the best rate I've got. I'm not going to tell you how to spend it, but I would think that'll cover a down payment and some inventory to get you started."

Forget peanuts. I needed a vendor to show up with champagne!

"Two fifty sounds good," I said.

"Great. It'll take me about an hour to fill out the paperwork, but I won't have the check ready until tomorrow. Okay?" It was the middle of the afternoon, and the promise of the money I needed felt like a hypothetical, not a reality. Pete added, "I'll write you a promissory letter right now if you're afraid I'll change my mind." He smiled.

I smiled back. "That would be lovely," I said. He typed in a few details into his computer then pointed and clicked and signed the paper that came off his printer. He tri-folded it and slipped it into an envelope.

I left the bank feeling a combination of nausea and enthusiasm. This was the single biggest favor anyone had ever done for me, and of all the people to owe, I had Nasty at the top of the list.

We were halfway between the bank and our cars, but I stopped walking and held Rocky in place. "I didn't expect that to be so easy," I said.

Nasty turned to me. "You did good in there," she said. "I expected a hundred, maybe one fifty. You made the difference."

"One week ago, his decision was a hard no. I had a prospectus and client testimonials, and none of it mattered. I don't know how to thank you."

"You don't have to thank me. Just pay off your loan."

"Why did you do this?" I persisted. "It's not just because you could."

"Because more women need to move the money around this town," she said. "And I know two things about you that make you interesting. One"—she held up her index finger—"you love what you do. And two"—she held her thumb out—"I'm the last person in the world you want to owe. Right now, you're probably trying to figure out how to pay the loan off in record time."

"I'm not that shallow," I said.

"Madison, if I wanted to, I would have offered you the loan myself. Standard terms and a higher interest rate than you just got from the bank. All I did was sit in a chair and smile at a loan officer."

She did more than that, and we both knew it. We parted ways, and I watched her drive off long before I pulled out of the lot. If I was wrong about Nasty, then what else was I wrong about?

33

My first phone call was to Dennis. "I want to put in a counteroffer on the property next door," I said when he answered. "This is Madison Night," I added.

He sighed. "We've been through this already. I'd love to sell you the property, but you don't have the resources."

"I do now. I've just secured a loan from the bank. Draw up the paperwork."

I returned to Mad for Mod and spent the next several hours working alongside Virginia and Imogene. By the time the sun set, Tex's temporary store was ready to go. Joanie loaned us fixtures from her store, and Mickey was the muscle that carried them in and moved them around until I felt the arrangement was right. At one point Virginia left then returned with a stack of framed images of pin-up girls in western attire.

"We use these at Jumbo's on theme night."

"This is a men's store," I said in consternation.

"Exactly." She carried the stack past me.

Sometimes, I found, it was good to acknowledge when you were out of your element and allow the experts some leeway. A few seconds later, I overheard Mickey exclaim, "Nice art. This store is awesome!"

I found Imogene in my office madly typing on her laptop. "I'm changing my entire work in progress. What do you think about Westerns? John Wayne meets Agatha Christie. Is that a thing? Can I make it one?"

I charged my iPod and plugged in my Square then gave her pretty much the same advice Joanie had given me. "You can make it be anything you want."

THE LAST TIME Tex and I spoke, he was going to check on the dean. Neither one of us mentioned that the dean had motive to dislike Professor Gallagher, and depending on exactly how ample the motive was, dislike could have escalated to murder. It was one thing for Tex to be at Hugo's house while the dean was passed out in his bedroom, but under other circumstances, things could go very wrong very fast.

But the one thing I couldn't do while setting up the store was call Tex. Unless he reprogrammed his phone, too, my name would show up. If the dean saw it, he'd question how well we knew each other, and even if Tex ran with a story about us studying together, it would be too close to the truth. This had nothing to do with keeping our relationship a secret —it had to do with keeping a murder suspect in the dark.

Tex had his hands full with this case. For once, I could support his investigation in a way that was necessary but not dangerous. I needed a way to turn over the keys without contacting him directly.

Oh, what the heck.

Nasty answered on the third ring. "What's up now, Madison?"

"Can you meet me at my showroom on Greenville Avenue?"

"When?"

"Tonight. Now. Or soon."

I heard rustling. "Ten minutes." She hung up.

I admired Nasty's communication style. She had freed herself from "please," "thank you," and "I'm sorry" and went for the more direct *Dragnet* approach with just the facts. True to form, she pulled into the lot behind the studio ten minutes later. It was almost as if she'd been parked around the corner and set a timer.

She entered through the back door. "What is this?" she asked. She moved through the now packed interior and ran her hand over fixtures filled with men's suits, shirts, and ties. Lots and lots of ties. We'd arranged things by size and signed them accordingly, and on top of each fixture was a hat on a stand. The rest of the hats were arranged on the rusted-out Platner table that had been taking up space in my shed out back. The rust, though not desirable to a mid-century modern enthusiast, fit right into the western-themed store.

She turned to face me. "Not that this isn't impressive, but you're a decorator, not a men's retailer."

"Means to an end," I said. I pointed at the front door. "Go outside and look at the window."

She did. When she returned, she nodded. "Where did the inventory come from?"

"Me." I paused for a moment. "And the property next door

to my house. My practice of buying estates and cherry-picking them for mid-century decor pays off yet again."

"You had this stuff all along?"

"Except for the hats, which are on loan, the clothes have been in my attic. I've sold cartons off over the years, but sometimes I just put the furniture and knickknacks in my storage locker, put the women's clothing in my closet, and left the rest to be dealt with later."

She nodded her head. "This is all a favor for Tex?"

"It started that way. Then it occurred to me that there was a way for me to benefit too."

She smiled. "Now you're thinking like a businesswoman."

I briefed her on the key situation and the reasons why I couldn't give it to Tex myself. She took it and agreed to complete the handoff. We'd come a long way from the days when I thought of her as my competition, though the more I got to know her, the more I recognized why Tex had found her attractive in the first place. It had less to do with her bombshell looks and more with her brain. I'd probably never shake the vestiges of jealousy that had first sprouted years ago, but there was a reason I kept calling her for help. I threw the lock on the front door, and we walked out the back together. She locked up, and that was that.

Nasty's silver Saab was parked next to the pick-up truck. She pointed at it. "You never did tell me why your car was at police impound."

"It was vandalized. Same parking structure as Professor Gallagher, same vandalism. A couple of details made it different, but still it was enough to raise suspicion."

Her forehead scrunched. "What was your car doing in the college parking structure at night?"

"I was at Kanin's Restaurant." I waited a beat and then added, "It was bongo night."

"I heard about that place. Did anything unusual happen while you were there?"

I tried to keep a straight face. "Define unusual."

"Did you have a good time?"

"We were surrounded by tipsy college students. My date got drunk and hit on Tex's date. My credit card was declined thanks to my recent loan applications. 'Good Time' is an oversell."

She had the look on her face she got when she was cataloging information to be retrieved later. Some people might have called it suspicion. Finally, she said, "You pack more into a day than most people get into a month."

I hadn't even told her about sleeping on the floor of the building next to my house. "Life is short. You never know when the rug's about to get pulled out from under your feet."

"I guess you know that better than most."

She unlocked her car and got in. I thought of something to ask her and tapped on her window. She lowered it. "Were there any scandals when you went to school?" I asked.

"There are scandals everywhere. Just depends on how far people are willing to go to hide them."

"If I were to look for scandals at Van Doren, where would I start?"

"Does Barbara still work the admissions desk?"

An image of the officious office manager popped into my head. "Yep."

"She's the eyes and ears of that school. If I had questions, I'd start there."

Nasty went one way, and I went the other. A brief recap with her had framed things in a whole new light. I kept trying to force unconnected information into a neat picture, but it got me nowhere.

I drove home and let Rocky out before I let us both in. The pull-down stairs were folded back up, but the second floor smelled like moth balls.

I opened the windows and let a breeze in. We were entering my favorite time of the year in Dallas. The temperature dropped at night, and each day, the air was increasingly drier. Come October, wardrobes would shift from T-shirts to sweaters. Tonight, a playful breeze blew at my sheer curtains, tossing them into the room and then sucking them back out. I took advantage of Nature's room freshener and went room to room, throwing windows open and airing the place out.

Tex called me at eight. "Thanks for the key. Nasty said you outdid yourself."

"I had help." Still, it felt good to hear the secondhand compliment. "How's Dean Wallace?"

"Not well. I'd be surprised if he shows up to teach class tonight."

"You don't think this was all an act, do you? An excuse for him to not show up so he got a head start leaving town?"

"Sounds like something Imogene would put in her book." He chuckled. "Hugo Wallace is hung over. I recognize the signs. When I got there, he was in bed holding an ice bag to his head."

"What about your hangover cure?"

"He was all out of ramen."

I didn't question the path to genius. I carried my cell phone down to the kitchen and put him on speaker. "Am I going to see you later?"

"Not tonight. I just got the results on your car from the

forensic automotive guys. The only thing in my future is a pot of coffee."

"Too bad. Virginia taught us a couple of dance moves today, and I thought you could critique my form."

"You're killing me, Night."

A DAY of cut classes had provided a temporary reprieve from school, but on Wednesday morning, I dressed in a white Orlon cardigan trimmed with a green leaf motif, a matching mint green skirt, and a sleeveless, wrinkle-resistant white blouse underneath and headed to campus. I was less motivated by the pursuit of knowledge than a desire to speak to Barbara. I picked up two lattes and an assortment of donuts, parked in Lot B, and went to the Canfield Building.

I timed my arrival to fall during eight o'clock classes, when most students were eating breakfast or still in bed. My plan worked. I approached the desk, and Barbara glanced up, offered a tight-lipped smile, and went back to punching holes in a stack of paper.

"Good morning, Barbara," I said. I set the donut bag on the counter and removed one of the cups from the cardboard tray. "I brought you a latte and donuts."

"I don't take bribes, thank you."

"Have you seen Dean Wallace yet today? I wanted to talk to him about my course load."

She made a great show of halting her task in progress. "Ms. Night. What you and the dean do in your spare time is your business. Don't expect me to make it mine."

"Me? And the dean?" I asked. "I think you have the wrong idea."

"This school used to have rules about students and faculty."

"I would think that's a good rule," I said. "Especially at a place focused on higher learning."

"If people just behaved themselves—" She stopped speaking abruptly. "I suppose it's none of my business. People are going to do what people are going to do."

Barbara, for all her efficient office manager qualities, seemed to see and know more than she wanted to see and know. Or perhaps she did want to see and know it so she could pass judgment.

"Dean Wallace and I spoke about my time here at Van Doren and whether it was the right move for me. The last time we talked, I said I wanted to think it through over the weekend."

Her expression changed. In a moment, she went from stern battleax to understanding grandmother. Her chest rose and fell with a short breath that seemed to fit her new attitude. She moved her hand from the hole punch to my hand, and squeezed in a supportive gesture. "You're a lovely student to have here. I wish we had more students like you. But I can understand what happened to Professor Gallagher has given you a bad experience."

"I admit it shook me up," I said, not sure where she was going. "A lot of what I see around here is unexpected."

"Yes, well, if it helps you with your decision, then you should know I don't support faculty members having relationships with students. *Any* students. What happened to Professor Gallagher was unfortunate, but he brought it on himself."

34

Barbara's mention of the murdered professor caught me by surprise. "I barely knew Professor Gallagher," I said. "I met with him to get approval to take his course, and then we had one class. And then—"

"Yes. We all know that 'and then.'" She shook her head. "I never liked that man, not when he came here and pressed for an office, not when he demanded the bookstore stock his book, and especially not when he started spending time behind closed doors with female students." She slammed the now-filled binder shut. "That is *not* the Van Doren way."

Barbara, in all her bluster, confirmed Faye's story. It lacked the details of time, place, and identity, but she knew the professor had had relations with students. I didn't like that Tex had so easily dismissed this angle, but facts were facts. I could hardly tell Barbara the autopsy results, and in this case, his vasectomy wouldn't prove anything.

I offered her the latte and donuts again, and this time she patted her waistline and declined. She was a blockade of militant energy, an illusion that would shatter if the students saw

246

her biting into a glazed apple fritter. She accepted the latte and moved it to her desk, and I turned and left.

It was a quarter to nine. This was the time slot for Professor Gallagher's class before the dean moved it. I wandered through the hallway with no clear agenda, eventually stopping in front of room 102. The room was empty, and I let myself in.

The last time I'd been in this room had been the night Ling pulled me out. That was also the night the dean put Tex on the spot and suggested the hat store would make a good field trip. I dropped my backpack into a chair by the front door and walked past the chalkboard, where I'd scribbled out the word Risk. The dean hadn't added anything to the board. Nor had anyone bothered to erase it.

Our lesson took place in discussion form. The aggressive teaching style of the murdered professor—the one that singled me out and used my business failure as a teachable moment—was no longer part of the curriculum. Yet that class had set me on the course I was on now. Expand. Go Big. Double Down. Take Risks.

I felt the loss to the students and to the college. I didn't like what I'd learned about Professor Gallagher, but the students were adults. Faye hadn't been angry about what happened with him, just sad that he wasn't around anymore. It didn't fit with the stories of sexual harassment or of him assaulting her in the parking structure.

I sat in my old seat in the front of the class, but having my back turned to the empty seats behind me felt vulnerable, so I got up and sat behind the teacher's desk instead. It tipped at an angle that felt like I was going to fall backward. I kept one hand on the worn wooden desk then, after I fully accepted the chair wouldn't flip, put my feet up on the edge of the desk. It was a power position: staring out at thirty wooden desks, thirty students who wanted to hear what the person in this chair had to say. Thirty people who wanted to get something from this class, though not all of it related to the curriculum.

A roar of applause sounded from the room next door. It startled me enough that I jumped, shifting my feet from the desk to the floor, tossing papers in the process. After I collected myself, I recognized the projected voice of Ansel Benedict quoting lines from *My Fair Lady*. Even with his classroom soundproofed, his voice penetrated the walls.

I bent down to retrieve the papers now scattered on the floor. It was Professor Gallagher's original syllabus. Some of the more controversial lectures had been lined out, and unrelated handwritten notes had been added on the side. One said *Wednesday night field trip to hat store.* That had been set up not by Professor Gallagher but by the dean. I assumed the handwriting was his, but I could find out sure enough by heading back and asking Barbara. I tucked the syllabus into my backpack and left.

My timing wasn't great. I'd spent longer than anticipated in the empty classroom, and now the halls filled with students. I sat on a bench in the hallway and observed the energy of youth as students mingled, laughed, flirted, and complained.

Octavio, my classmate from Radical Business Strategy, dropped onto the bench next to me. "Our class was moved to night," he said. "You remember that, right?"

"Of course, I remember that," I said, and then I added, "I wanted some quiet time to study, and I figured the classroom would be empty."

"So you're not dropping the class? I heard a rumor you were."

"From whom?" I asked instinctively. For all the gossip I'd expected, I hadn't expected any of it to be about me.

"Eric. He said he overheard you talking about it at a club over the weekend."

I'd started the gossip myself. "I'm considering it," I admitted.

"Don't," he said. "I took this class to learn something different, and the best part of class was when we talked about your business. That first day when you walked in, I thought you were in the wrong place. You don't exactly look like a businessperson."

"What's your point?"

"I don't look like a businessperson either," he said. "My uncle owns a landscaping company, and my whole family expected me to go work for him. I have tendonitis from playing baseball all my life, but I don't want to let them down. Thanks to you, I saw I could write my dad a business plan for expansion." He held up his notebook. "I have twenty ideas of how to get the word out and bring in new clients."

"That's great," I said.

"Yeah, but Dean Wallace is all about moderate growth and safety measures. He keeps trying to sound like he's teaching us Gallagher's syllabus, but he doesn't get the material."

I thought back to the manuscript pages Tex and I found at Dean Wallace's house. If it were originally his content, then the material should have been second nature to the dean. It seemed taking over the class had given him the perfect platform to illustrate *he* was the leader in the field, not the prof who had inspired the students with his concepts of radical thinking. But if Dean Wallace were the fraud and Professor Gallagher knew what he was doing—

"Would you recognize Dean Wallace's handwriting if you saw it?"

"If it's a C- or a D+, I would."

I pulled the syllabus I'd found in the classroom out of my bag and handed it to Octavio. He glanced at it. "That's it. See what I mean?" he said, indicating the notes on the page. "He crossed out the best parts of class." He handed me the paper, and I put it away. "Don't drop the class," he said.

"I haven't decided what I'm going to do," I said, "but either way, you're welcome to visit me at my showroom any time." I pulled out a business card and handed it to him. "I like the principles of radical business strategy more than I anticipated."

Octavio pocketed the card. He looked up at hallway. "I gotta run or I'm going to miss my next class. See you at the hat store tonight?"

"Maybe," I said.

I watched him tuck his books under his left arm and weave through the thinning crowd of students, feeling mildly guilty about lying. I'd probably never see him again.

I refolded the syllabus and placed it between the pages of my copy of *Rad Rage*. Like the welcome I'd received after my first day of class, Octavio's unexpected compliment felt good. I pulled the syllabus back out and flipped through the book pages to find the chapter we were expected to discuss next.

"Eliza," said a boisterous voice. "You're looking lovely today."

I used the syllabus as a bookmark and looked up. Today Ansel wore an unseasonable tweed suit with suede elbow patches, a dress shirt, and an ascot. "Hello, Henry," I said. "How's the rain in Spain?"

"I believe that's my question." He bowed slightly. "But I do appreciate how you let me stay in character." He dropped onto the bench next to me. "I've been trying to impress upon my students the need for an actor to connect with the material. Look at the world through the character's eyes. Understand their motivations. It's an easier lesson to experience than to teach."

"Costumes help," I said, nodding at his attire.

"That is the lesson I attempted to instill in them today, but as with many things in life, seeing and doing aren't the same."

I stared at the suit he wore. It was mid-fifties, well-made. "Have you heard about the pop-up vintage menswear sale this weekend?" I asked. I gestured to his suit. "Clothes from the forties through the seventies. My business class is taking a field trip there tonight. Your class might enjoy it, too, for entirely different reasons."

His eyes sparkled. "A pop-up vintage menswear sale? My theater group would be interested. Who's promoting it?"

"Rexford Allen," I said tentatively. I was treading in dangerous waters. "If I see him, I can have him come by your office."

"No need. I'll get his contact information from Barbara. Thank you for the tip, Eliza." He shared a genuine smile and said goodbye.

I didn't regret the effort put into Rexford Allen's Stetsons and More because it didn't matter if Tex planned to maintain his cover. I owned the inventory (minus the hats); his claim to the business was in name only. One big blowout sale, if promoted correctly, could give me a jumpstart on my first loan payment. What I needed were flyers or a way to promote the thing. Right now, word of mouth was the best thing I had going.

Unsure where things stood with my course load, I slipped

into the back row of Decision-Making for the Business Leader and set my backpack on the floor behind the seat in front of me. The professor was talking about making decisions. Eric stood off to the side, leaning against the wall. The professor continued, and Eric watched the lecture hall as if gauging interest in the subject matter.

Instead of taking notes, I sat back and listened. It was as if the professor were describing me. Before I recognized what I was doing, I raised my hand. The professor took a moment to notice. He pointed at me. "You in the back row. Question?"

"Is it possible to make a wrong decision?" I called out.

He repeated my question for the benefit of the class. "Is it?" he asked, this time looking to the class for feedback. A couple of heads nodded, and one guy in the front said something about the circumstances.

The professor leaned back against the wall. "Simple answer: no. It is not possible to make a wrong decision."

Rumblings of dissent rippled through the two-hundred-student audience, and a few hands went up. The professor looked at me. "Do you know why?"

"Because every decision is a step forward," I guessed. "It is taking the business to a new place. And every time you take your business to a new place, opportunities arise."

He pointed at me but looked at the class. "Yes. Did you hear that?" he asked them. "Every decision takes a business to a new place. Is your job as a business owner to manage your business? No. That's what a manager is for. A leader's job, a business owner's job, is to keep the business moving. And the way to do that is to decide. Every crossroads: decide. Every day: decide. Every minute: decide. Choose to change things. Experiment. Innovate. Shift. Take risks. Leading is not comfortable. Leading is not making friends. Leading is not making your employees happy, or content, or secure. Leading is inspiring people every day with new ideas, and new ideas come from one place: decisions."

The student next to me leaned over. "Nobody ever asks questions in a lecture hall," she said. "Thanks."

The professor asked the class to turn to page one forty-three in our textbooks. I hadn't brought mine, so I relaxed while the rest of the class shifted around and pulled them out.

The doors to the back of the lecture hall opened, and two campus police officers entered. They descended the stairs in the aisle between the center and right side of the room, and the closer they got to the front, the louder the ripple of whispers from the audience. As they reached the front, they said something to the professor. He turned to Eric.

Eric dropped the stack of papers he held and took off. He ran up the left-hand side of the lecture hall, taking the steps two at a time. The campus police didn't chase him. He charged through the doors at the back of the auditorium.

I was in the back row on the other side, and without thinking, I jumped up and left. Whatever assistance I'd hoped to contribute was unnecessary. Additional CPs were in the hall outside of the lecture hall, and Eric was in their custody. The same campus police officer who'd answered the call when Gallagher died in his car instructed him to face the wall with his hands up. He put handcuffs on Eric's left wrist, pulled his arm down behind his back, then pulled his right arm down and cuffed it too.

Eric turned his head. "What are you looking at?" he asked me.

"I can't believe it was you," I said.

"You don't know anything," he said. He shrugged away from the CPs, and they escorted him out of the building.

I watched as the group of men in uniform walked away. It felt anticlimactic. Where were the police sirens? Where were the homicide cops? Where was the reading of the Miranda rights, the proclamation of charges against Eric, or his inevitable claim of innocence?

Two CPs remained behind. One pointed at the class. "Were you in there?" he asked. I nodded. "How many students?"

"About two hundred."

This time he nodded and then looked at the clock on the wall. "Give it an hour and see how fast word spreads. Of course he couldn't be in a twenty-student class this morning."

"You could have waited."

"Couldn't take a chance. The evidence came in this morning, and we knew we had him."

The doors to the lecture hall opened, and students flooded the hallway. I stepped out of the way with the CP and watched as curious onlookers searched for signs of gossip they could report to friends and roommates later. Thanks to the swift action of the campus police, Eric was already out of the building.

"He seemed so driven," I said.

"That was the problem. He and his friend got greedy. They've been running a credit card scam from local restaurants, charging against open balances then pocketing the difference the companies write off." He shook his head. "Apparently one of the professors here threatened to turn him in, and he vandalized the professor's car as a message. I guess none of that matters now."

"I guess not," I said slowly.

3 5

THE COLLEGE KEPT THE NEWS OF ERIC'S ARREST QUIET. IT WAS an unusual end to an unusual case that I'd been closer to than I thought. My credit card had been linked to the scam being run from Kanin's, but I'd been savvy enough to demand the card's return. I'd overheard a portion of an incriminating conversation outside the venue yesterday, and I now wondered if I'd be expected to make a statement or testify.

If the student gossip could be trusted, then Eric's friend, the bartender, had been the one to suggest sending the professor a message by vandalizing his car. A five-hundred-thousand-dollar profit from one night was enough motive for the two students in question to send the professor a warning. I must be getting jaded, because my first thought was that I'd seen people kill for less.

I remembered how Eric hung out at the admissions desk and how he used the door at the back to leave. I told the police about hearing a door slam before I spoke to Gallagher that first time and how Eric could have easily gained access to spike the professor's coffee. It was conjecture on my part that fit the narrative. It was up to the Sues to either gain a confession or find evidence to support the theory.

Being anywhere other than where I was expected to be felt suspicious. I double-checked that my phone was on silent, and I made the rounds through Ethics, Accounting, and Statistics.

As much as I wanted to meet up with the Radical Business Strategy class at Tex's fake store, I doubted I should. Hugo thought I was dropping the course, and Eric's absence would trigger gossip amongst the students. I hadn't heard from Tex, so I didn't know whether he'd canceled the field trip or was juggling the added pressure of showing off his store to maintain his cover. It was a perfect storm of comedy and tragedy, and I wanted no part of it.

It was quarter to seven by the time I left the Canfield Building. The sun was on its descent, and a warm glow of dwindling rays coated the quad. A sparse crowd wandered across the lawn, most of them heading toward the cafeteria. Sweatshirts and denim jackets had been pulled over T-shirts. Dallas's version of autumn was right around the corner.

I hoisted my backpack over my shoulder and headed toward the parking structure for what might be the last time. Tomorrow, I would pick up my check at the bank, and from there, I'd set my business plan in motion. I'd learned more from a few short lessons at Van Doren College than I could have wallowing in my circumstances, but I wasn't equipped to sit around in a lecture hall when I could work on reopening Mad for Mod instead. I was halfway to the parking structure, lost in thoughts of Nelson bubble lamps and Noguchi coffee tables when I heard my name—or rather, the name I'd come to know was meant for me.

"Eliza." Ansel Benedict jogged toward me. "I'm glad I caught up with you," he said. "Are you walking to your car?"

"Yes."

"Let's walk and talk." He dropped into step next to me. "I spoke to your classmate. Rexford? He said you were the one running the menswear sale this weekend."

"He did?" Tex had said nothing about making that public knowledge, though if his case was solved, there might be no further reason for his cover. He was going to owe me double if the entire execution of the store now fell on my shoulders. "We discussed it briefly, but nothing was decided," I added, attempting to be vague.

Ansel waved his hand as if the details didn't matter. "I don't care who's running the event. I'd like to arrange a private sale ahead of time. Perhaps tonight?"

"Tonight won't work," I said. "My Radical Business class is there on a field trip."

His forehead creased, and his thick black eyebrows almost touched. "But you're here. Why would you be here if they're on a field trip?"

Now that I'd made the decision to myself, it was easy to say out loud. "I'm dropping the course. The whole program." We walked side by side for a few wordless steps. "Van Doren is a good college, but it isn't for me."

"That's a shame," he said. "I'll miss seeing you around the campus, but we must all follow our chosen paths."

We entered the parking structure. It was darker than usual. The truck on loan from Mickey was parked next to a small black Mercedes. A row of lights nearby cast the two vehicles in shadow. I was happy to have accepted an escort from Ansel even if he was more mild-mannered than most. The parking structure creeped me out.

As we approached the cars, Ansel pulled out his pipe. A piece of red and white striped fabric fell to the ground and landed next to my sneaker. He bent down and scooped it up and then shoved it back into his jacket pocket, but not before a sense of familiarity washed over me.

I'd seen that fabric somewhere before. I'd seen more fabric in the past two days thank I had in months thanks to the cartons of clothes from the store next to Thelma Johnson's house and the menswear I used at Tex's store. Yet there was something familiar about it—

"Well, I suppose this is our goodbye," Ansel said. He held out his hand. "Eliza?" He reached out and tapped my arm with the hand not holding his pipe. "Are you okay? You look like you saw a ghost."

I directed my attention to his face. "How did you know this was my truck?" I asked.

"There are two cars in the parking structure, and the other one is mine," he said. He held both arms out, indicating the lack of other vehicles around us, which did make these two stand out in contrast. "And you *did* lead the way."

"I suppose I did," I said. I reached into my backpack and pulled out my keys, then shifted them to my left hand and held out my right. "It was a pleasure meeting you, Ansel—I mean Henry."

He took a deep breath, and his chest puffed out. He put his pipe between his lips and extended his hand, and I shook. The moment of contact, a flash of memory pierced my mind. The fabric. The rag. It was the same as the rag that had been shoved inside Gallagher's tailpipe the ay he died. Ansel had had a length of it on his desk the day I wandered in looking for Gallagher. The day he showed me the prop starter's pistol and started calling me Eliza. I'd been distracted by his theatrical manner and had written it off as him cleaning his pipe.

Realization must have crossed my face the moment my suspicions became clear, because Ansel tightened his grip around my hand. I matched the pressure to keep my fingers from becoming crushed. I forced a smile to my face. "You know, maybe I should meet up with my class on their field trip after all," I said. "One last hurrah, as they say."

He kept his hand tight around mine. I tried to pull my hand away.

"Ms. Night, there's no need to panic," he said. He smiled malevolently. "You're really not my type."

It was an odd thing to say. Ansel spoke in theater quotes and character, though the scene felt less *My Fair Lady* and more *Silence of the Lambs.* His type? What Broadway play was that from?

A new thought entered my mind. The animosity Ansel had shown toward Professor Gallagher and how he'd gone so far as to have his classroom soundproofed so the neighboring prof couldn't overhear him. He hadn't said anything about the neighboring class. It had been about Gallagher. Why would he care if the professor next door could hear him? He'd care if he used his classroom for something other than classes.

"You like college girls," I said suddenly. "That's your type, isn't it?"

He shrugged. "The heart wants what it wants," he said. "The last one shouldn't have played hard to get."

"Who?" I asked.

He continued as if I hadn't spoken. "And he shouldn't have gotten involved."

"Professor Gallagher?" I asked.

He shook his head in disgust. "A professor thinks he can threaten me to change how I approach life. I take inspiration where I can find it." He gestured to the air with his fingertips up, as if summoning his muse on the spot. "Sometimes inspiration comes from a song or a piece of poetry. And sometimes it comes from a blond coed."

"You're the one who tampered with Professor Gallagher's car," I accused. I matched Ansel's conversational tone and said it in a voice far calmer than I felt.

He smiled. "It is amazing what one can get away with when one dresses in costume. A professor with car trouble gets noticed. A mechanic working on that same car flies under the radar."

"But he died," I said. "You killed him."

"He wanted to kill my spirit. He threatened to go to the board of directors and report my relations with those girls. He left me no choice."

Competing warnings and questions made it difficult for me to think clearly. Ansel was off somewhere else, temporarily, and despite my not being his type, the danger of being alone with him in the parking structure at the end of the day was palpable.

I opened my mouth to speak and silently hoped my voice wouldn't shake when I did. "Thank you again, Ansel. Break a leg at opening night."

I gave him the full wattage of my smile. His smile faltered momentarily and then returned. He patted the back of my hand with his left hand and then released me. I climbed into the truck. Ansel closed my door behind me. I slammed the locks. He disappeared around the back of the truck.

An acrid smell irritated my nose. I pinched it closed. My eyes watered. I'd roll down the window as soon as I was away from him. The smart move was to get to a public place and call campus police or Tex or 911. Every one of Tex's warnings played through my head.

I put the key into the ignition. The floor mat was flipped up, and as I reached down to put it back into place, I noticed something odd. A small round hole in the floorboards. I ran my fingertips over the opening and felt the edges of a plastic tube.

It was how Professor Gallagher had died. The exhaust had been diverted into the cabin of the car. Ansel Benedict was the murderer. I had my proof, but I was trapped.

I dumped my backpack onto the passenger seat and grabbed my phone. The smart call would be to 911. I called Tex instead. "It's Madison," I said. "The killer is Ansel Benedict. He sabotaged the truck, and I'm trapped in the parking structure with him. I don't know if I'm going to make it." I felt tears streaming down my face. "I love you too."

3 6

Starting the engine felt like imminent death, but remaining inside the cabin with the windows up wasn't smart either. Ansel walked away from my truck and climbed into the small black Mercedes. He started the engine, backed out of his space, and drove away.

He was overconfident. I watched his taillights as he drove toward the lot exit. The ticket booth would be closed, but he would still have to wave his ID in front of the scanner to get the gate to retract. I looked at my phone and willed it to ring. It didn't.

I jumped out of the truck and went around back. The wad of striped rag from Ansel's pocket was jammed into my tailpipe. I hadn't started the car, so the pipe was still cool. I bent down and pulled it out then checked to make sure there were no other obstructions. I ran my fingers around the inside of the tailpipe, feeling for a drill hole. I felt nothing. He'd done something to the truck, but I didn't know what.

Anger boiled up within me. There might have been a heat flash in the mix; at this point, it was hard to tell.

I climbed back into the truck and turned the key. I leaned across the passenger-side seat and opened the door. Fresh air filled the cabin. I left the doors open and backed the truck out of my space and then called 911. "There's been an accident in parking structure B of Van Doren College. Right by the exit. I don't know if anyone's been hurt."

And then I put the truck in gear. I hit the gas. I accelerated until the truck rammed into the taillights of Ansel Benedict's small black Mercedes.

A moment after impact, the airbag deployed and blocked my view. It took a moment for my wits to return. I blinked a few times and shoved the door open, gasping for fresh air. I saw movement in the car in front of me. Ansel's airbag must have deployed too, but unlike me, he seemed more concerned with restarting his car and driving away.

I unhooked my seatbelt and fell from the truck to the pavement. The rag I'd pulled out of my tailpipe landed by my hand. Acting on autopilot, my fist closed around the wad, and I crawled to Ansel's car. I jammed it into his tailpipe, burning my fingers. I leaned against the front bumper of my truck and put the sole of my shoe against the end of his tailpipe to keep the rag in place. All I wanted to do was keep the engine from starting until the police arrived.

A campus police golf cart appeared on the drive and headed toward us. This was my cavalry? My chest heaved as I inhaled and exhaled the fresh nighttime air. A siren sounded in the distance and then another and another.

That was more like it.

"HE CONFESSED," Tex told me.

I sat in a red leather armchair of anonymous design provenance while he doctored the cuts along the bridge of my nose and left cheekbone. We were at Rexford Allen's Hats and More. The class had long since left. After giving my statement first to campus police, second to Ling, and third to the insurance agency, I got checked out by a medic while arrangements were made to tow Mickey's truck to police impound. I called the cab driver who had driven me home Saturday night and he shuttled me from the school to my store. It was a good thing my Alfa Romeo was ready to be picked up; I doubted Mickey would loan me his Mustang now.

"Just like that," I said.

"Not exactly. A student came forward and leveled accusations against him. Sounded like a Harvey Weinstein sort of thing. She found out she was pregnant and confided in Gallagher. When he was murdered, she got scared. She thought if she talked, he'd kill her too."

"Faye," I correctly guessed.

Tex nodded. "She didn't know about Gallagher's vasectomy, so when she found out she was pregnant, she chose to pass it off as his."

"If you release the findings of the autopsy, her secret will become public."

"My goal is to convict a killer, not drag a victim through the mud. I'll see what I can do."

He added to the story. The assault took place in Gallagher's office when Faye first went to see Gallagher during office hours. She confided in him, and he confronted Benedict—though not for the reasons you'd think.

"Faye said there were others. I'll set up an interview station at the campus to try to get statements."

I thought about how Faye was afraid to tell her family

about what happened, but had confided in me. "When you did that deep dive into Gallagher's past, you said there were accusations of this sort of thing against him at the last school where he taught."

"Right. Gallagher wasn't thrilled about Ansel using his office for the same thing that got him canned. If someone made noise, Gallagher would make a convenient scapegoat. Benedict laid back and observed Gallagher long enough to see he was talking to Faye. He also saw the ongoing vandalism that Eric and his friend perpetuated on Gallagher's car."

"So the vandalism and the tailpipe weren't connected," I said. "But Benedict wanted it to look like they were."

Tex nodded. "Your car gave us a big clue. The dean was with me the whole time, so it couldn't have been him."

"But the manuscript pages, what was that about?"

"Credibility. With Gallagher gone, Dean wanted to pass off the ideas as his own."

"You can always deputize me if you need some help."

"Not a chance, Night." He put a butterfly Band-Aid across a cut on my forehead and then, in an uncharacteristic display of affection, leaned down and kissed it gently. He didn't lecture me or deny I'd made a difference in the outcome of the case because he couldn't. We worked well together, despite all the reasons we shouldn't. I'd learned to go with the flow.

I SPENT the next several days getting ready for the weekend sale. Tex blew his cover in a meeting with Hugo, which had the added side effect of getting me credit for the entire Rexford Allen store. Not that it mattered, since I'd already decided to leave the MBA program. I staffed the pop-up with students from my Radical Business Strategy course, offering them either $20 per hour in cash or $30 per hour toward start-up capital for their own businesses. Only one took the cash.

The sale, as I expected, was a rousing success. We drew a local crowd from our last-minute newspaper and radio ads, and Bill's Western Warehouse sent clients our way too. Employee of the Month went to the small gray cat Joanie and I had rescued who was on the road to recovery. She knocked over a pair of cowboy boots, which initiated a domino-like chain reaction. The pair on the end landed at the feet of the owner of Southfork Ranch, who bought the whole lot. By the end of the day, we named the cat Calamity.

I made enough for the down payment on the building next to Thelma Johnson's house. Mad for Mod was officially expanding to a second location. In the first fifteen minutes of a class on radical business strategy, I'd come up with the business plan that I put into motion today.

When the story broke about Ansel Benedict's role in William Gallagher's death, a slew of people came forward with stories about both men. Hugo joined the fray, claiming he and Gallagher had discussed co-writing a follow-up to *Rad Rage* called *Fury Road,* but out of respect for his colleague, he chose to abandon the project. Whether true or not, we'd never know since Gallagher wasn't around to contradict him.

Two weeks later, I received a piece of mail that tied the whole experience up with a neat bow. It was an official package from Van Doren College. I set the rest of the mail on the kitchen table and went to my newly renovated sitting room. Tex and Mickey had loaded in a blue tweed sofa, and, sticking with the astronaut theme, I downloaded and framed an image of Earth from NASA's archives taken by John Glenn on his Mercury Mission. A plush, ivory rug contrasted nicely with the warm pine walls and the sofa, and a table lamp with globe lights provided a second bright counterpoint.

I put Doris Day's *Day by Night* album on the turntable and opened the package. Inside was a letter that said, based on a review of my business skills and ties to the Dallas community, I'd been nominated to receive an honorary MBA. The board of the college had approved the nomination. Since the timing of the approval did not line up with a regular graduation schedule, my diploma was included in the package.

I slid a leather-bound folio out of the padded envelope and opened it. A yellow Post-It had been stuck to a sheet of clear plastic that protected the official document, and on the Post-It was this message:

This one requires a thank you. – Nasty

I ran my fingers over the embossed text on the diploma. I might not look good on paper, but my name sure did.

Want more Madison? Preorder *The Kill of it All*, Madison Night Mystery #9, coming February 2022!

ACKNOWLEDGMENTS

Thank you to the readers of the Madison Night Mysteries! I'm constantly delighted that a quirky mid-life amateur sleuth who wears clothes from the mid-century found her audience. A special thank you to the subscribers of the Weekly DiVa, especially those who volunteered to be dead people. Your responses made my day. Chosen for this book are Tootie Morgan, Gwendolyn Yeary, Tony Yanuzzi, and Moira Graham. Never fear, though, I'll need a fresh crop of volunteers for the next book!

Thank you to the Polyester Posse for your ongoing support, and to Amy Ross Jolly for your early thoughts on this manuscript. To my writing group: Ellen Byron, Lisa Matthews, and Gigi Pandian: your brainstorming and support is invaluable!

There's an oddball cast that inspires each Madison Night Mystery, (thought they often have no idea Madison Night exists), and Teacher's Threat was no exception. Thank you to the following people who inspired elements of Madison's business school experience: Scott Galloway, Adam Grant, and Mr. Wonderful.

And, of course, no Madison Night Mystery would exist without the magic of Doris Day. Thank you for your spirit, joy, and determination.

ABOUT THE AUTHOR

National bestselling author Diane Vallere writes funny and fashionable character-based mysteries. After two decades working for a top luxury retailer, she traded fashion accessories for accessories to murder. A past president of Sisters in Crime, Diane started her own detective agency at age ten and has maintained a passion for shoes, clues, and clothes ever since. Subscribe to the Weekly DiVa, to get girl talk, book talk, and life talk, at www.dianevallere.com/weekly-diva.

The Kill of it All

<u>Sylvia Stryker Outer Space Mysteries</u>

Fly Me To The Moon

I'm Your Venus

Saturn Night Fever

Spiders from Mars

<u>Material Witness Mysteries</u>

Suede to Rest

Crushed Velvet

Silk Stalkings

<u>Costume Shop Mystery Series</u>

A Disguise to Die For

Masking for Trouble

Dressed to Confess

<u>Mermaid Mysteries</u>

Tails from the Deep

Murky Waters

Sleeping with the Fishes

<u>Non-Fiction</u>

Bonbons For Your Brain

www.ingramcontent.com/pod-product-compliance
Lightning Source LLC
Chambersburg PA
CBHW071747190726
48292CB00003B/898